Book One: The Diamondback Ranch Series

The atmosphere sizzled in the small office. Jessie stood like a statue, her eyes opened wide. "Why did you come back?" Her raspy voice held a note of accusation.

Cameron also heard anguish in her words. Was he causing Jessie pain? When all he wanted was to hold her in his arms, take her to bed and make love to her until the passion between them was spent?

In two long strides, he was beside her. She backed against the file cabinet. He stepped closer.

"You know why I'm back. We need to finish what we started seventeen years ago." He touched a finger to her cheek, traced the smooth line of her jaw, eased his hand behind her neck and pulled her to him. Her trembling intensified and she put her hands on his chest as if to ward him off.

He caught her hands and moved them over his heart. "Feel my heartbeat, Jess. It's beating for you." He pressed his body against hers. "Feel how much I want you. I tried to stay away, but God help me, I couldn't."

His mouth claimed hers in fierce desire. Jessie moaned, holding back only for a second, knowing deep down resistance was hopeless.

She couldn't help it... she kissed him back.

D1733338

Reviews for Anne Marie Novark

"Ms. Novark is a fantastic storyteller, and has a wonderful grasp for writing very emotionally charged scenes. There is far more here than a romance, but rather, this is a story with complexity and substance, which is everything a reader could ask for and more."

~ **Fern, *Long and Short Reviews***

"This is the first book I have read by Ms. Novark but it will not be my last. Her characters are strong and passionate and she takes the reader along for an emotional ride through her story!"

~ **Steph B., *The Romance Studio***

"I loved reading a western romance that wasn't historical. I've heard that everything is bigger in Texas, but didn't think that would mean the sex scenes as well. Get a tall glass of lemonade since this book is hot!"

~**Robyn, *Once Upon a Romance Review***

The Doctor Wears a Stetson

The Diamondback Ranch Series

Book One

Anne Marie Novark

THE DOCTOR WEARS A STETSON

Second Edition

To all of those who have been given a
Second Chance at Love...

PROLOGUE

"*Y*ou want me to do *what?*"

Jessie Kincaid dropped the wrench she'd been using to tighten a loose radiator hose on an old pickup truck. The metal tool echoed on the cement floor of her father's service station. She stared toward the big double doors, wondering if she were hallucinating.

"I want you to go to the prom with me." The deep low voice drifted into the garage on the cool West Texas breeze.

Jessie's head buzzed and her lungs refused to draw in air. Had Cameron McCade, star football player for the Salt Fork Bulldogs, the most popular senior in school and drop-dead gorgeous, just asked her to the prom?

Oh my God. I'm only a freshman.

Nothing like this had ever happened before. Her life was predictable, boring. Every afternoon, she came home from school, changed into her coveralls and helped her dad. She repaired cars, trucks and tractors, pumped gas, changed oil and some days even balanced the books. Kincaid's Garage did a brisk business, considering it was one of two gas stations in the small town of Salt Fork, Texas.

Jessie took a deep calming breath and stared at Cameron. He was still standing near the garage doors looking incredibly handsome in his Stetson, with his hands stuffed in the pockets of his letter jacket.

"Will you go with me, Jess? Please?" He walked toward her until he was only a couple of feet away.

His killer smile made Jessie's stomach flutter. She picked up the wrench and placed it in the toolbox. "Why me?" she asked, although she knew the answer.

Cameron's sapphire blue eyes widened in surprise. He probably hadn't expected her to question his invitation. Jessie knew he had recently broken up with his girlfriend. The prom was only a week away. Everyone had arranged for dates and escorts months ago, everyone except Jessie.

"Why not you?" Cameron asked, tipping back his Stetson and smiling down at her. "Don't you *want* to go?"

That smile was dangerous. Cameron was dangerous, too. He was way out of Jessie's league. She didn't date much; hardly ever, if you wanted to get downright technical about it.

"Okay. Sure, I'll go with you." Who cared if she was his last-ditch effort? A chance like this didn't come along every day.

Cameron nodded. "Good. I'll pick you up around

seven on Saturday. See you, Jess. And thanks."

She watched him drive away, knowing she probably had a dopey grin on her face. Just like all the girls in town, Jessie had a crush on Cameron McCade. Except her feelings bordered on hero-worship, because he was so far beyond her reach. Never in her wildest dreams had she thought she would actually get to go out with him.

Oh my God.

When her heart finally stopped pounding, she ran to find her dad and begged him to take her to Lubbock to buy a dress. She hadn't worn one since she was a baby. They went that night and after a long and frantic search, she settled on an ankle-length, backless gown of creamy white satin.

On Saturday afternoon, Jessie locked herself in her room and prayed for a miracle. For the first time in her life, she rolled her hair, painted her nails and applied makeup. Donning the dress, she looked at herself critically in the full-length mirror on the back of her bedroom door. Not miraculous, but definitely not bad.

Jessie grabbed her new purse and went in search of her father. She found him in the office next to the garage, seated at his desk with his back to her. She stopped in the doorway, suddenly feeling nervous and unsure. Was her dress too daring? Her hair too curly? Had she used enough makeup? Too much? She didn't want to embarrass Cameron.

"Dad, close your eyes before turning around," Jessie said. "I want your honest opinion of how I look."

George Kincaid swiveled until he faced the doorway. Slowly he opened his eyes. A glowing smile spread across his rugged face. "Come on in, baby. Let me have a closer look."

Jessie stepped into the small office and pirouetted in front of him. She watched his face anxiously, trying to decide if she could trust his judgment. He was her father after all.

"You'll be the belle of the ball," he said. "Just like your mama, God rest her soul. Cameron McCade is one lucky fella."

"Oh, Daddy. You know he only asked me because he and Patti broke up and no one else was available."

"Even if you weren't his first choice, he's still lucky," her father declared stoutly.

A knock on the office door made Jessie jump. "Goodness! He's here!" she cried.

While Cameron shook hands with her father, Jessie looked him over. He was stunning in his black tuxedo and baby-blue shirt. The tanned face, clear blue eyes, and that kilowatt smile were producing astonishing effects on her. How was she going to survive this night? She wished with all her heart she had more experience with boys.

Cameron turned toward her. Jessie summoned a brave smile, banishing the urge to run away. He didn't say anything for a moment. It was his turn to look her over, from the top of her head to the tips of her brand new satin slippers, and then slowly back up. He inched closer, his gaze appreciative. "You look nice."

"Thanks." His compliment warmed her all over. "So do you."

Jessie's father cleared his throat. "Cameron, you take

care of my little girl, you hear? Don't keep her out too late. Have a good time, baby." He kissed her cheek, before disappearing into the living quarters behind the garage.

Cameron thrust a small cardboard box toward her. "I forgot to ask what color your dress was going to be. I hope this is all right."

Jessie opened the box. Nestled in the folds of tissue lay a wrist corsage of pink tea roses. "It's beautiful."

Cameron removed the flowers and took her hand in his. "May I?" His voice sounded low and husky in the confines of the office. Before she could reply, he slipped the elastic loop over her trembling hand.

Jessie admired the corsage, sniffing the delicate fragrance, closing her eyes. This whole experience was like a dream or fairy tale. Not real at all.

"Are you ready to go?" Cameron asked.

That deep voice again. One more sniff of her corsage and Jessie opened her eyes. "Not yet. Stay here, I'll be right back."

Dashing to the kitchen, she opened the refrigerator door and grabbed the single blue carnation wrapped in clear cellophane. Thank goodness one of the older girls at school had explained about corsages and boutonnières, because she never would have thought of it herself.

When she offered the flower to Cameron, he shook his head. "Huh-uh, it's your turn." He stepped closer until he stood only a few inches away.

Jessie gulped and prayed she wouldn't faint. Nothing had prepared her for the incredible sensations flowing through her body. This was unknown territory where unfamiliar emotions threatened to consume her. She was very good at taking apart engines and putting them together again. She wasn't good with boys.

"Pin it on, Jess."

With shaking fingers, she carefully fastened the boutonnière to his lapel with a long straight pin. She avoided eye contact, keeping her attention on the task. The warmth from Cameron's body, the width of his shoulders, the clean fresh scent of his aftershave made Jessie feel weak in the knees. If she had known being close to Cameron would cause her to lose her breathing abilities and the control of her muscles, she never would have accepted his invitation to the prom.

Yeah right. She wouldn't have missed this for the world. Everything was new and exciting and just a little bit scary.

The drive to the high school gym took all of five minutes. Somehow, Jessie managed to get out of the truck with some semblance of grace. She wasn't used to dresses and high-heels. Cameron adjusted her satin wrap around her shoulders and escorted her inside.

Everyone gaped at Jessie when she walked in the gym on Cameron's arm. No one could believe *she* was attending the prom with Cameron McCade! A feeling of pure feminine satisfaction rose inside of her, giving her confidence a much-needed boost.

"Cameron! Jessie! Over here."

Cameron guided Jessie to one of the center tables, where Lester Smith stood waving to them.

"Hey, buddy." Lester slapped Cameron's shoulder.

"I grabbed the best table and saved a place for you two."

"Thanks, Les." Cameron seated Jessie before sinking his tall frame into the chair between her and Lester's date, Amanda Harding.

He threw his arm across the back of Jessie's chair. When his fingers brushed back and forth against her shoulder, her body tensed. The soft caress made her tummy feel heavy and tingly at the same time. If Cameron's touch affected her so strongly, how was she going to survive dancing with him?

"Hooey, Jessie!" Lester let out a low wolfish whistle. "You sure look a danged-sight better in that dress than you do in coveralls. Don't she, Cam?"

"Yes, she does." The admiration in Cameron's deep voice made Jessie's cheeks burn, and she didn't know where to look.

The noise in the gym quieted when the band struck up the first tune. Amanda dragged Lester to the dance floor. Jessie laughed at the comical look he threw Cameron.

All desire to laugh ceased when Cameron pushed back his chair and stood. "Shall we join them?" He gave her one of his special smiles and held out his hand.

The heat from his fingers burned her flesh as he led her to the dance floor. How in the world was she going to survive when Cameron held her in his arms for the slow dances?

For the first two sets, the band played rock and roll. Jessie enjoyed moving to the music. She loved to dance. But then the beat changed, the tempo mellowed and the time of reckoning had come. Cameron pulled her into his arms and held her close. They swayed to the soft music of a love song. She held herself rigid, afraid to breathe, afraid she'd do something foolish.

"Relax," Cameron whispered in her ear.

Jessie forced herself to ease her strained muscles. She tentatively laid her head against Cameron's chest and sighed deeply. This was like a piece of heaven.

When Cameron suddenly stiffened, Jessie jerked her head back and looked up at him. He was staring at something or someone across the gym. She quickly scanned the dancing couples and found the object of Cameron's fierce gaze. Near one of the doors, Patti Nichols and Bubba Garrison were locked in an intimate embrace. Jessie wasn't familiar with the details of the big break up, but Cameron certainly wasn't happy with his ex-girlfriend's behavior.

He forced a smile when he caught Jessie's look of concern. "Sorry about that." With a shrug, Cameron turned with the music and held her close.

The rest of the evening passed in a dreamy blur for Jessie. Cameron never looked Patti's way again. Instead, he focused all his charm and attention on Jessie. She, in turn, lost her heart.

When the prom ended, Jessie and Cameron walked out into the starry West Texas night with Lester and Amanda.

Lester had his arm around Amanda's waist, whispering in her ear, making her giggle. He punched Cameron's arm. "Some of us are going up to Lover's Point. Why don't y'all come along?"

Jessie, acutely aware of Cameron's big hand on the

small of her back, tried not to panic. *Lover's Point?*

Cameron glanced down at her before answering. "I don't know, Les..."

Amanda laughed nastily. "I bet Jessie's never been to Lover's Point. Her experience with parked cars is strictly mechanical."

"Unlike yours. Right, Amanda?" Cameron said.

Amanda sputtered, caught Lester's arm and hurried away.

Cameron helped Jessie into the truck and braced an arm on the doorframe, searching her face. "Why don't we go for a little while? We don't have to stay long," he said softly. "It's up to you."

Jessie swallowed hard. Did he really want to take her to Lover's Point? Was he offering her a way out or himself?

Amanda's words stung. Jessie raised her chin. "I guess we can go if you want to."

He stared at her for a moment, then nodded. She trembled at the thought of being alone with Cameron in the parked truck.

Lover's Point was a large precipice overlooking a deep gorge west of town. After maneuvering his truck on the bluff, Cameron dimmed his headlights and rolled down the windows.

Jessie hoped she didn't look as nervous as she felt. When Cameron swung his arm over the back of the seat and turned toward her, it was all she could do not to open the door and run.

"You should wear a dress more often." Cameron's deep velvet voice oozed over Jessie's heart, causing it to miss a beat. He gently caressed the nape of her neck and his muscular thigh pressed against her own, the satin fabric of her gown offering little protection from the heat of his body. When had he moved so close? And why?

Oh my God, he's going to kiss me.

Good lord, what was she doing on Lover's Point with Cameron McCade? She had never kissed a boy in her whole entire life. She had no idea how to go about it. Did it come naturally? Was there a certain technique or skill to it?

Cameron leaned toward her, his eyes on her lips. A husky laugh from one of the cars floated on the warm breeze. Jessie felt Cameron's body go rigid as he stared at the couple in the next car. She knew without a doubt it must be Patti and Bubba.

Before she could turn to look, Jessie was locked in a vise-like embrace. Cameron's lips came down on hers hard, demanding. He forced her mouth open, plunging his tongue inside, grinding his lips against hers until she thought she would smother.

Jessie realized Cameron was hurting and angry. She felt an overwhelming need to give him comfort. But the punishing force of the kiss frightened her, and she tried to push him away.

Immediately, the kiss changed. The pressure of Cameron's lips gentled and Jessie stopped struggling. Abruptly, he released her.

She opened her eyes slowly, then quickly closed them again. All traces of fear had faded, replaced by a vague flickering of desire. Her breasts felt heavy and full. A churning sensation began in the pit of her stomach and traveled all the way to her toes. It was a new and intoxicating feeling.

"Look at me, Jess."

Gripping her hands in her lap, she peeked up at Cameron. His sexy blue eyes were fixed on her face. Jessie's stomach ricocheted and she looked away.

Cameron cupped her chin, forcing her to meet his gaze. "You've never done this before, have you?"

She felt her cheeks flood with color. "No."

"Was that your first kiss?"

Jessie nodded miserably.

Cameron slammed his palm against the back of the seat, making her jump. He stifled a curse. "I'm sorry, Jess. I shouldn't have done that to you." He raked his fingers through his hair. "I don't know what's wrong with me. I've been acting like a jealous jerk all night long. Hell, *I* was the one who wanted to break up with Patti."

He reached for Jessie and gathered her in his arms again. He traced her lips with a thumb, and she shivered in response.

"Let's try this again," he said. "A first kiss should be something special."

The sound of Cameron's voice, his gentle touch, and his breath on her cheek–all were threatening Jessie's control. She had already had her first kiss, thank you very much. She wasn't sure she liked it.

Cameron tightened his hold on her. His heartbeat both comforted and excited her. "I'm going to kiss you, okay?"

Jessie had barely nodded before his mouth took hers

a second time. This kiss was very different from the first. It had nothing to do with jealousy or anger. Cameron was kissing her for her own sake. Her world turned upside down.

Slowly, she raised her arms and clasped them around Cameron's neck. He adjusted their position, cradling Jessie closer into his shoulder.

The kiss deepened and soon turned into a sweet wild passion. Jessie hung on for dear life, allowing the exhilarating feelings to consume her. Cameron pushed her backward until she was lying flat on the seat.

Jessie gloried in the feel of his big body covering her. She drew the powerful shoulders closer until his chest rubbed against her breasts. She hadn't worn a bra with the halter-topped evening gown. Every movement produced exciting new sensations.

Just when she thought she might die from the exquisite torture, Cameron pulled back. He stared down at her, his breath rasping in his lungs. He quickly sat up, bringing Jessie with him.

Still lost in a fog of passion, she reached for him, but he caught her hands and shook his head. "No more," he said, keeping her away.

Jessie tried to gather her wits as she straightened her gown. She didn't want to look at Cameron, but she *had* to look at him; she had to say something. "I think you better take me home."

Cameron gripped the steering wheel. He was still breathing hard, and his eyes glittered hotly. "I'm sorry, Jess. I didn't mean to take advantage of you. You're a special kind of girl. Don't ever change." He reached across the cab and traced her lips with his thumb again.

"You're too young, too damned young," he said. "I'm leaving for college after graduation. I have to get out of this town, Jess. Away from the ranch. I want to be a doctor. I want to help people. I want to heal them, make them better. I've planned my future and I'm never coming back."

Jessie nodded in understanding; he was leaving and taking her heart with him. She lifted her chin. "You know, you're not the only one with a plan. I'm going away to college, too, when it's time. I want to major in journalism and work for a newspaper some day."

Cameron smiled and flicked her nose. "Not going to be a grease monkey all your life?"

"No, I want to write," she said. "And I don't want to live in Salt Fork forever, either."

Cameron started the truck. "Thanks for going with me, Jess. It was fun."

She swallowed the lump in her throat. "Yes, it was."

The drive home was silent. Cameron pulled around to the back of Kincaid's Garage, where the porch light glared yellow in the darkness. He led her up the walk.

Jessie opened the screen door and turned toward Cameron. This was it, then. The end. Her fairy-tale prom night was over. "Thank you for a wonderful time," she said, holding out her hand, feeling like a fool.

Cameron stared at her hand, then at her. His face was taut, as if he were in pain. His blue eyes burned like jewels. Jessie wondered what was wrong.

Suddenly, he reached out and pulled her to him, arching her slender body into his. "I have to have one more kiss, Jess. One... more... kiss."

His mouth crushed down on hers. This wasn't an obligatory goodnight kiss, Jessie thought, her heart hammering in her chest. This was a kiss like you read about in novels or watched at the movies. He must feel *something* for her, or he wouldn't be kissing her like this. How was she going to stand it when he left forever?

Cameron broke the embrace and set her away from him. "Good bye, Jess." He didn't look at her again, didn't turn to wave. He got in his truck and drove away into the night and out of her life.

CHAPTER ONE

Seventeen years later...

*J*essie Devine needed a miracle and the sooner the better. Only a miracle would keep her from losing the service station and garage she'd inherited from her father. She loved the business and hated to think she might lose it. With taxes and insurance coming due, plus a mountain of medical bills still waiting to be paid, not to mention everyday expenses that were eating her lunch, money was a top priority and a commodity she sorely lacked. No matter how she tallied the columns on the spreadsheets, the numbers just wouldn't add up. She'd been working late every night for the past two months.

Face it, Jess. You're flat broke.

With a sigh, she set to work once more, crunching the numbers on the computer screen, comparing them to the ones in her account book.

The roar of a powerful engine outside the station jerked her attention from the spreadsheets. With a frown, she glanced at the ancient clock hanging on the wall. *Good lord, it was nine-thirty.* Who could be stopping by so late, when she was obviously closed? No one from Salt Fork, that was for sure.

Peeking out the window, she saw a shiny black Jaguar with the hood up and a large man leaning over the engine. A Jaguar in Salt Fork? A stranger in distress, no doubt about it. She tucked several loose strands of hair under her baseball cap and decided to investigate.

Jessie's pulse accelerated as she neared the stranger and the Jaguar. What wouldn't she give to service a car like that? The thought of working on that engine sent shivers down her spine. Her fingers itched to explore and repair. With her eyes glued on the expensive sports car, Jessie didn't realize the stranger had come forward to greet her until she heard his deep voice.

"Hello, Jess."

Her head snapped toward the man, and Jessie found herself gazing into familiar blue eyes. *Oh, my God. Cameron McCade.* Her heart shifted gears and her lungs stalled in her chest.

What was *he* doing back in town? He'd been gone a long time. Now suddenly he was standing only a few inches away, his musky aftershave triggering old memories. Ancient memories. It had only been one night, one night many years ago.

A sharp October breeze brought Jessie back to her senses. Summoning a smile, she extended her hand, thankful to see it steady. "Hey, Cameron. Wow. I sure didn't expect to see you here."

"It's been a while, hasn't it?" he said, taking her hand in his.

When his strong fingers closed over hers, Jessie swallowed hard. She remembered Cameron's touch... oh how she remembered.

"Yes, it's been quite a while." Quickly, she withdrew her hand and walked over to inspect the car. There was so much to say. Or maybe there was nothing to say at all. Perhaps he didn't remember.

Jessie ran an expert eye over the engine. "Looks like the fan belt snapped and the radiator's overheating. Have you driven all the way from Houston?"

He moved closer to get a better look at the steaming radiator. "Yeah, I've been on the road since early this morning."

When he brushed against her shoulder, Jessie stiffened at the close contact, shocked by the sharp jolt of awareness coursing through her veins. The heat from his body penetrated the thick cloth of her coveralls, making her insides turn all squishy. Cameron McCade had always affected her that way.

Dragging in a deep breath, she fought for control. Her reactions were ridiculous. She was thirty-two years old, for crying out loud. Not fifteen, like before.

Cameron quickly stepped away, and Jessie wondered whether he was also feeling the electricity crackling between them.

"It's been one hell of a trip," he continued smoothly, slipping his cell phone from his belt. "I blew a tire early this afternoon and wasted two hours getting that taken care of. And now the damn car is overheating. I'll have it hauled to Lubbock tomorrow. Dallas or Tyler can pick me up tonight." He started punching in numbers on his phone.

"Don't call your brothers," Jessie said. "I can drive you out to the ranch. It's on my way home." She didn't know why she'd offered, but when he smiled, her heart revved up a notch and alarm bells clamored in her brain, reminding her of the danger of Cameron's smile.

At eighteen, he had been boyishly good-looking. Now he absolutely stole her breath away. Tall and powerfully built, he had broad shoulders and a muscular neck. The wavy brown hair, strong jaw line, and hint of dimples when he smiled... oh yes, a deadly combination.

Cameron hooked the phone back on his belt. "I'd sure appreciate a lift to the ranch, if it's not too much trouble. I really hate to bother Dallas. He's probably already in bed, since he wakes up before dawn."

"No trouble," Jessie said. "You can pull your car into the garage, and we'll get you to the ranch in no time." She ran to the office, shut down her computer, grabbed her keys and locked the door.

While Cameron parked the Jaguar, Jessie sat and waited in her old Ford pickup truck. *Cameron McCade.* She still couldn't believe it. Since leaving for college, he'd only returned once or twice a year to visit his family at the Diamondback Ranch. He'd stopped by her station a handful of times to buy gas, but hadn't come near her in the last few years. She'd often wondered why.

Jessie gripped the steering wheel tightly. Cameron McCade had been the golden boy in high school. Everyone in town had admired him, herself included. He'd been three grades ahead of her and completely out of her league.

Jessie's thoughts flittered away when Cameron climbed in the pickup and set a duffel bag on the seat between them. "I locked the garage doors," he said, buckling his seat belt. "The Jag should be safe."

She nodded, trying not to hyperventilate from Cameron's close proximity. "I'm sure it would have been okay where it was," she said. "But a car like that attracts a lot of attention, and I wouldn't want to tempt anyone."

She shifted gears and started down the main drag. The street and stores of the tiny town were deserted, with only a couple of cars parked under the water tower. A group of teenagers stood talking and laughing. Everyone else had closed shop and gone home.

"Some things never change," Cameron said. "Doesn't seem that long ago, it was me talking and joking with friends under the water tower."

"It's always been a popular hangout." Although, Jessie had never hung out there. Then again, she'd never been one of the popular ones.

Soon the lights of Salt Fork were behind them. Darkness surrounded the truck on the lonely highway. The domed night sky spread from horizon to horizon heavily sprinkled with tiny pinpoints of light. The full moon hung suspended against the blackness, huge and yellow and bright.

Cameron leaned forward and stared out the windshield. "Damn, the stars are beautiful. You can't see near this many in Houston. The lights from the city make it impossible."

Was that regret she heard in his voice? "Just one of the many benefits of living out in the middle of nowhere," she said.

"You enjoy living here, don't you?"

"It's my home. And yes, I do enjoy living here. Unlike you." Good lord, had she really said that out loud?

"Yeah, unlike me."

Out of the corner of her eye, Jessie saw Cameron frown and try to stretch his legs, but there wasn't room. He settled by leaning his head against the glass of the rear window. "It's good to be back, though," he said.

"You've been gone a long time."

"Too damned long."

Again Jessie thought he sounded regretful. "It's been over a year since you've visited the ranch. Ruth sure has missed you."

"I know. Mom's been on my case big time. I usually don't wait so long between visits, but this past year has been hectic and I just couldn't get away."

Jessie kept her eyes on the road, trying to ignore the cramped confines of the truck. Every breath she drew filled her lungs with Cameron's masculine scent, the musky aftershave that had embedded itself in her brain a long time ago. She tried not to inhale too deeply.

"Ruth told me you were busy at the hospital and were up for a promotion. Seems like all of your plans have worked out."

Cameron shifted in the seat. Jessie sensed his pent-up energy, that restlessness that had haunted him all his life.

"I got the promotion–"

"That's wonderful!" Jessie said, wondering at his lack of enthusiasm. "Congratulations. You've worked hard for it, I know."

"I've worked my ass off. If I decide to accept it, I'll be working even harder."

"*If?*" Jessie asked, not believing her ears. "Why in the world would you hesitate? It's what you've wanted, isn't it? Ruth keeps me up to date on you and your progress. She's very proud of you. Wow. Head surgeon at M.D. Anderson. That's a big accomplishment, Cameron."

He dragged a hand over his face. "Yeah, thanks."

Cameron didn't say anything more and Jessie glanced at him, then away. "So... I'm guessing you're here for Ruth's birthday?"

He took a deep breath and once more tried to adjust his position on the hard bench of the truck. "Good guess. It's the big six-o. Couldn't miss that, now could I? Mom's party promises to be the party to end all parties, if Tori has her way."

Jessie smiled. "Your sister usually gets her way, doesn't she?"

Cameron smiled back. "Yeah, she does. You going to be there?"

His low sexy voice oozed slowly over Jessie like motor oil on a piston cylinder. She was aware of his eyes on her, looking her over. Oh yes, the man was dangerous, his smile lethal.

"Of course, I'll be there. Your mother invited me a couple of weeks ago when she brought her car in for inspection. She didn't mention anything about you coming home, though."

Cameron shrugged. "I didn't know if I could get away from the hospital until a couple of days ago."

"Is that when you found out about the promotion?"

He nodded. "My boss–the man I'd be replacing, my mentor–insisted I take time off to think about it and decide. It's a big step."

"And one you're not sure you want to take?"

"Sounds crazy, doesn't it?"

"You never were one to jump into anything without a lot of planning."

"I've always been the man with the plan."

"That's what they called you in high school," Jessie said.

"Just like they called you grease-monkey."

Jessie smiled at the old nickname. "Right."

"But I understand that's not all you've been doing," he said. "Mom keeps me updated about you, too. I hear you're on the Chamber the Commerce. The president, no less."

"I got elected last year. More like coerced. It was a unanimous decision."

"Hey, that's great. You really are involved in the community."

And why wouldn't she be? "This is home, Cameron. Salt Fork may be a small town, but I want it to be the best it can be. I sit on the city council, too. That's how I'm getting the new medical facility built here. Did Ruth tell you about the clinic?"

"She mentioned something about it."

"Maybe while you're here, I can give you a tour. I could use your opinion about a few things."

"Sure, Jess. I'll help anyway I can."

When he called her 'Jess' in that deep baritone of his, her tummy fluttered like when she was a kid. She gripped the steering wheel tighter. "How long are you staying?"

"Only until Monday. I have to get back to Houston. I don't have the luxury of more than a few days off at a time."

"Definitely not one of the perks of being a busy surgeon."

He swiped his hand through his hair. "You would not believe."

"But you like being a doctor?"

"Yes, very much. How about you? Still enjoy working at the garage?"

She smiled. "Yes, I do."

"I'm sure your dad would have been proud of you. Keeping the family business going. I know you must miss him."

Jessie nodded. "Desperately sometimes, even though it's been–gosh, eight years. But he was ready to go. He'd been fighting the cancer for a long time. At least I had time to say goodbye. Your dad died so unexpectedly, you didn't have the chance."

"Yeah. It's damned hard to lose a parent. Makes you

think about things. Makes you appreciate the parent who's left."

Jessie shook her head. "I wouldn't know about that. I barely remember my mom."

"Damn, Jess. I'm sorry. I spoke without thinking."

"It's okay. Don't worry about it."

He adjusted his position on the seat again. "I was sorry to hear about TR's accident."

Jessie swallowed a lump in her throat at the mention of her dead husband. Sorrow, mixed with guilt and regret. A whole lot of guilt and a whole lot of regret. "I still can't believe he's gone. It's been almost two years."

"You seem to be holding up all right. Keeping busy and all."

"Helps keep my mind off things." She took a deep breath. "Can I ask you a question, Cameron?"

"Sure. Ask away."

"Are you ever sorry you left Salt Fork? Do you miss the ranch? Don't you miss your family?"

"That's three questions, not one," he said with a smile.

"Math was never one of my strong suits." If it were, maybe she'd be able to crunch the numbers on the spreadsheets better. Only it wasn't the math that was the problem, it was the lack of funds. Best not to think about that right now.

"No, your strong suit has always been cars and engines," Cameron said.

"And don't forget tractors."

"Oh right, can't forget the tractors." Cameron was silent for a moment. "But what about writing? Weren't you going to go to college? Study journalism or something?"

How did he remember that? *She* remembered every detail of prom night–every word spoken, every kiss shared–but she hadn't expected Cameron to remember.

"Dad got sick my senior year. I couldn't go off and leave him," she said. "So I stayed and took care of him, drove him to Abilene for chemo treatments and kept the garage running. The medical bills were astronomical. I'm still trying to pay the last of them off. By the time it was all over, I was twenty-four. Too old to go to college or so I thought. Besides, I had the garage to consider."

"And that's when you married TR Devine."

He made it sound like she'd committed a mortal sin or something. And in a way, maybe she had. "TR was a tremendous help during Dad's illness."

"A good reason to marry someone. He was a lot older than you. Did you love him?"

Jessie felt like Cameron had slapped her. She'd thought he couldn't hurt her anymore. Boy, was she wrong.

"Of course, I loved him. But this isn't any of your business, is it?" she said, lifting her chin and gathering her defenses. She'd loved TR in a quiet, respectful kind of way. "And he wasn't much older. Only ten years."

"Ten years. That's quite an age difference."

She shrugged. "Like I said, it really is none of your business."

Cameron raked his fingers through his hair again. "You're right. I was out of line. I apologize."

They drove in silence along the highway for several

minutes. Jessie wondered at the tone of Cameron's voice. He sounded angry... almost... jealous. But how could that be? He'd certainly touched her young heart, the night of the prom. But she didn't think for a minute she'd touched his. He hadn't been able to leave Salt Fork fast enough after graduation.

Turning off the pavement onto a dirt road, Jessie kept the truck steady, deftly avoiding the deep ruts in the gravel surface. The headlights showed old tumbleweeds piled high against the barbwire fences, standing at attention like sentinels guarding the way.

The truck dipped as they crossed a gully and Cameron grabbed his bag before it fell to the floor. "Damn, this road is bad," he said.

Jessie dodged several loose tumbleweeds, hitting one or two that she couldn't avoid. "Probably something you haven't missed, huh?"

"No, I definitely don't miss the dirt roads."

"So what do you miss? You never answered my questions."

"Oh, I've missed a few things."

"Like what?"

"The clean fresh air, the Double Mountains, the stars at night and..."

Cameron turned his head, and she felt his eyes sweep over her. The cab of the truck seemed to grow smaller, more intimate. Jessie's body hummed with expectation. "And what?" she asked softly. "What else do you miss?"

He looked out the window again. "My family. I've definitely missed my family."

So much for expectations. "Do you ever regret

leaving?"

"I'm not sorry I went away to college. And I'm certainly not sorry about becoming a doctor, if that's what you mean. I enjoy living in Houston, for the most part. What I do regret is not coming home more often. I missed seeing my dad, missed saying goodbye, like you said. Mom's not getting any younger either. I wish I'd made more time to see her."

"Well, you're here now," Jessie said. "Ruth'll be ecstatic."

Turning off the road, they passed beneath the gates of the Diamondback Ranch, sixty-four hundred acres of prime farm and ranch land. Soon, the barns and ranch house came into view.

She'd always loved the sprawling old house Cameron's great-grandfather had built. Thick white columns graced the lighted front porch where four Shaker-style rocking chairs sat invitingly. The full moon cast its pale light over the house, completing the cozy picture.

Jessie pulled to a stop in front of the house, cut the engine and hopped out. Walking to the front of the truck, she removed a tumbleweed that had caught on the bumper.

Cameron retrieved his bag and came around to stand before her. "Thanks for the lift."

"No problem," she said. A liquid core of heat started building in the region of Jessie's midsection. She quickly stepped back and away from Cameron.

He advanced until she was almost wedged between him and the grill of the pickup. "Why don't you come inside?" he said. "Mom and Dallas will want to thank you for bringing me home. Tyler, too."

Jessie stared at the designer emblem on his polo shirt. The knit fabric stretched taut across his broad chest. "Thanks, but no. I... I can't stay."

The front door opened and a strong beam of light shot out into the yard. Dallas and his mother stood on the porch.

"Cameron, is that you?" Ruth McCade called. "Who's that with you? And where in the world is your car?"

"It's Jessie," he said over his shoulder. "My car broke down and she offered me a ride. I've invited her in, but she's refusing."

Jessie tried to stand straighter and bumped Cameron's iron hard thighs. The contact jump-started her body. A quick glance at his face showed awareness gleaming under heavy-lidded eyes.

She had to get away. She had to say something. "Cameron, I really need to go–"

"Jessie?" Ruth called from the porch. "Come on in, darlin'. You know you're always welcome at the Diamondback."

Jessie frowned at Cameron, who was trying to hide a smile. "You think this is funny, don't you?"

He shrugged and laughed.

Jessie leaned around him to answer his mother, hoping her voice wouldn't betray what her body was feeling. None of this was the least bit funny. "Thanks, Ruth. But it's getting late. I need to get on home."

Sidestepping away from Cameron, Jessie said, "I'm

leaving now."

He reached for her hand and dropped his car keys into her open palm, slowly closing her fingers, not letting go. "Why don't you take a look at my car and see what's wrong? Think you can handle it?"

The heat of his touch made Jessie gasp. She wanted to jerk her hand away. She wanted him to hold onto it forever. One thing sure hadn't changed since Cameron had left Salt Fork. Her body still responded to him like fire to gasoline. But she wasn't a kid anymore. She lifted her chin. "Sure I can handle it. There's nothing I'd like better."

He arched one eyebrow and smiled again. Jessie watched in fascination as two dimples played hide-and-seek on either side of his mouth. Those clear blue eyes glittered wickedly, and he tightened his hold on her hand.

"Nothing?" he asked softly.

The powerful yearning deep down inside shell-shocked Jessie. Pure desire pumped through her bloodstream. That one word was teasing, taunting. Did Cameron actually remember the kisses they'd shared? *Surely not.* A man like Cameron McCade wouldn't remember something like that.

"You two going to stand here all night?"

Jessie didn't know whether to be glad or disappointed when Dallas McCade walked up and took his brother's bag. The big rancher always intimidated her. Maybe it was the habitual frown on the man's face.

Cameron released her hand and grinned at his brother, slapping his shoulder in greeting. "Hey, don't rush me. I was saying goodbye to Jess."

"Well, hurry it up. Mom's waiting." Dallas turned and carried the bag to the house.

Cameron stared at his brother's back. "What's wrong with him? He didn't even say hello to you."

Jessie shrugged and shook her head. She wasn't going to explain Dallas's rudeness. Not here. Not tonight.

Cameron opened the truck door and waited for her to climb in. He closed the door and motioned for her to roll down the window. "I'll see you tomorrow... to check on my car."

Jessie nodded and managed a weak smile, gunned the engine and threw the truck into reverse. She needed to put as much distance as possible between her and Cameron McCade. Shifting gears, she stomped on the gas pedal and left a trail of dust behind her as she sped down the dirt road toward home.

CHAPTER TWO

Cameron watched the pickup plow down the road until it was out of sight. Who would've thought he'd still feel a sizzle of awareness for Jessie Kincaid? *Not Kincaid; her name is Devine. She's Jessie Devine now.* Not the pretty girl he'd taken to the prom, but a grown woman. A sexy and desirable woman.

The ride to the ranch had given him ample opportunity to study her as she sat behind the steering wheel. The cab of the truck had been dark; the greenish glow from the instrument panel the only light. But it had been enough.

Time had enhanced Jessie's beauty. The coveralls couldn't hide her slender waist, the outline of her breasts or the curve of her hips. Her wrists and hands were delicate, strong enough to work on engines, but delicate just the same. She had a pixie look about her with that small dimple in her chin. And her full lips were made for kissing.

Cameron remembered the dark night a long time ago, sitting in his truck with Jessie up on Lover's Point–kissing her until her lips were swollen, his body rock-hard. He hadn't thought about that night in years. But he thought about it now.

Damn! The kisses they'd shared had been incredibly hot, almost x-rated. He hadn't asked her out again because he'd instinctively known the attraction he felt for her could be detrimental to his plans.

Cameron turned and walked toward the front porch. He found that he wanted to kiss Jessie again, hold her in his arms. He wanted to see her out of those damned coveralls. He wanted to see her out of her clothes, period. Would she go out with him if he asked? Could they continue where they'd left off all those years ago up on Lover's Point?

Maybe a walk down memory lane with Jessie would help him with the decisions plaguing him. Career decisions. Life decisions. He was tired of the perpetual restlessness he'd never been able to shake. He needed to figure out what the hell he wanted to do with the rest of his life.

He stepped onto the porch. "Hey, Mom. How're you doing?"

"Oh, Cameron!" Ruth McCade welcomed her son with outstretched arms. "I'm so glad you're home."

"It's good to be home." He gave her a big bear hug and kept his arm around her shoulders as they entered the house.

"So, tell me," she said, patting his chest. "Did you

get the promotion?"

Oh man, the promotion. Something he should be thrilled about, but wasn't. "It's mine, if I want it. I just can't seem to make up my mind."

She patted his chest again. "Don't rush it, baby. Think it through. You're good at that."

Dallas met them in the hall on the way to the kitchen. "I put your things in your old room."

"Thanks." Cameron glanced around. "Where's Tyler?"

"There's an air show in San Antonio." Dallas rolled his eyes. "Need I say more?"

"Crop-dusting season's over, I take it?" Cameron asked.

"Yes, but you know Tyler," Ruth said. "Can't get him away from his airplanes."

"He won't be here on Saturday?" He might have to clobber his youngest brother if he missed their mom's party.

Ruth shook her head. Oh yeah, Tyler was cruising for a bruising. "No, but he sent me a box of my favorite chocolates and will be home next week. Come on, let me fix you something to eat. How about a piece of pecan pie?"

"Sounds good." He followed his mother and brother into the kitchen.

Dallas poured a brandy and sat at the old oak table. Cameron snagged a chair across from him and stretched his legs, easing the cramps in his knees. "So, what's been happening around here? Anything I should know about? And what the hell's going on with you and Jess?"

He took a bite of the pie his mother placed before him.

"Something's definitely going on," Dallas said.

"Between you and Jess?" He looked up from his plate, not liking the sinking sensation in the pit of his stomach.

"Hell no," Dallas said.

Relief rushed through Cameron. He didn't want to examine the feeling too closely. "Then what's up? What's the matter?"

"Copper River Oil Company is nosing around the Devine Place, that's what's the matter. Jessie has leased her mineral rights to them."

"So what?" Cameron asked. "That's no skin off our butts."

"Yes, it is. She's running short on cash."

Cameron took another bite of pie. "How do you know that?"

Ruth sat down at the table next to him. "Jessie told me. She's still swamped with medical bills from her father's illness and TR's accident and it's not easy running a garage in Salt Fork. Business isn't exactly booming here."

Dallas went to refill his glass of brandy. "Want one of these?" he said to Cameron over his shoulder.

"Yeah, pour me a double." He finished his pie and pushed the plate away. Leaning back in his chair, he crossed his arms. "So Copper River Oil is snooping over on the Devine Place. What's that got to do with us?"

"It's too close for comfort," Dallas said. "If Jessie's leased the rights on her place, what's to keep her from leasing them on ours?"

"She promised she wouldn't," Ruth reminded him.

Dallas handed Cameron his drink and sat back down. "I don't trust her."

Cameron looked at his brother. "Are you telling me, Jessie owns the mineral rights on the Diamondback Ranch? How did that happen?"

Dallas sipped his drink. "She owns one hundred percent of the mineral rights–"

"On the whole ranch?" Cameron asked.

"No, of course not," Ruth said. "Only on the sections of land near the Devine place. She inherited them from TR."

"How did the Devines end up with mineral rights on the Diamondback anyway?" Cameron wanted to know. "Did I miss something there?"

"You never did take much interest in the ranch," Ruth said.

"Aw, Mom, don't start that–"

"All right, I won't. Anyway, Grandpa McCade sold the rights to TR's grandfather forty years ago. The money helped buy the Gordon place and increase the size of the Diamondback."

Dallas got up and paced back and forth across the kitchen. "I probably don't need to worry," he said. "Copper River Oil won't want to drill there anyway. There's no oil. Grandpa leased the rights way back when, and they didn't find anything then. But if Jessie decides to lease, there's no way we can keep Copper River off our property. And with all the new technology, they may want to try again." He stopped in front of the table. "I don't want strangers on the ranch, tearing up the land. I'd have no control whatsoever."

"Jessie knows how we feel," Ruth said. "She promised not to lease and I believe her."

"I don't believe her. I want those mineral rights, damn it." Dallas sat back down.

Cameron swirled the brandy in his glass. "Have you offered to buy them from her?"

"Hell yes, I've offered. She refuses to even talk about it."

Ruth picked up Cameron's plate and walked over to the sink. "Jessie told me she couldn't sell them. She made a promise to TR on his deathbed." She dropped the plate in the sink with a clatter and snapped her fingers. "Wait a minute! I just thought of the perfect solution. *Cameron* can persuade Jessie to sell them to us."

"Me?" He jumped up, almost knocking over his chair, and stared at his mother, not liking the odd gleam in her eyes.

"Sure," Ruth said. "Jessie always asks about you when I stop by the garage. I think she's still sweet on you. And she's been alone for a long time. She hasn't dated much since TR died."

Cameron turned toward Dallas. "Help me out here."

His brother shook his head. "Don't look at me. You know how Mom is once she's on a roll."

Ruth frowned at her oldest son, then gazed at Cameron again. "It's very simple," she continued. "All you have to do is ask her out and use your irresistible charm on her."

"What irresistible charm?" Dallas said with a snort.

Ruth wiped the table with a damp cloth. "The

irresistible McCade charm, of course. All of you boys have it. Tori has it, too," she said proudly. "All Cam needs to do is turn it Jessie's way, and I'm sure she would agree to sell the mineral rights to us."

Cameron sat down again. "Damn, Mom. Why don't I just ask her to marry me? That would bring the mineral rights back into the family and save Dallas time and money."

Ruth clapped her hands in delight. "What a wonderful idea! I'd love to have Jessie for a daughter-in-law. I already think of her as a daughter. And if you married her, that would make it even better. But do you think she'd accept? She likes you and all, but marriage? I don't know..."

"Mom, I was joking," Cameron said. "Look, I've already decided I want to ask Jessie out while I'm home. If she accepts, I promise I'll talk to her about the mineral rights. That's all I'm willing to do, though."

"But Cam, I'm sure Jessie would marry you," Ruth said. "She likes you a lot."

"Lord, help us from matchmaking mothers," Dallas muttered into his glass.

Ruth swatted him with the washcloth. "Hush, or you'll be next."

"Okay, okay. Geez, don't hit me again," he said, scrunching his shoulders away.

"Then don't be a smarty mouth," Ruth said, folding the washcloth. "I just want my children to be happy, that's all. I want to see y'all settled down, married and happy. Is that too much to ask?"

Cameron smiled. He'd heard this spiel countless

times before. "What about all the grandkids you want us to produce?"

Dallas groaned. "For God's sakes, don't encourage her."

Ruth sat back in her chair with a dreamy look in her eyes. "Grandkids will be the icing on the cake."

The next morning, Cameron parked Dallas' pickup across the street from Kincaid's Garage. He crossed the two-lane highway and came to a dead stop near the gas pumps. The large double doors stood wide open and he could see two people leaning headfirst under the hood of his car. Two pairs of legs and two bottoms faced the street. One of the bottoms drew Cameron's attention. *Very nice.*

Tight blue denim outlined the lush feminine shape. The worn fabric hugged the delicate curves. For some reason, Jessie hadn't worn her coveralls today. Cameron glimpsed a line of bare flesh above the waist of the jeans, where she had tied the tails of her plaid shirt. He admired the long legs, the shapely bottom and the smooth skin. From the moment he'd seen her last night, he couldn't get her out of his mind.

Cameron walked purposefully toward the garage. He cursed under his breath when he realized most of the engine was out of the car and lying scattered on the greasy floor. What was Jessie doing? It had only been a broken fan belt, for Christ's sake. He leaned on the side of the car and cleared his throat.

Jessie's head popped up. "You're early," she said, her green eyes narrowed. She had a smudge of grease on her nose and looked pretty damned cute in that ball cap she was wearing.

"It's almost lunch time," he said, barely resisting the urge to wipe the smudge away, which would just be an excuse to touch her.

"You're kidding, right?" She frowned at him. "Is it really that late?"

The man standing beside Jessie chuckled. "Jessie loses track of time when she's engrossed in her work. She gets in the *zone*." He snatched a rag from his pocket and handed it to her. "Here, you have grease on your nose."

"Oh great." She blushed and quickly wiped off the smudge.

Cameron clenched his teeth and raised an eyebrow at the man. "And you are?"

The stranger took his time wiping his hands, then extended one in greeting. "Sam Garza," he said. "I work for Jessie. Fantastic car. We've never had a Jag in here before."

Cameron shook Garza's hand. He didn't like the idea of Jessie in such close contact to the man. He didn't like the feelings bombarding him, either. "I thought a fan belt broke last night. Have you found something else?" He glared at the engine parts on the floor.

Sam glanced quickly at Jessie. Cameron was surprised when her cheeks flushed crimson, as if she were embarrassed.

"We didn't think you'd be here so early," she said,

wiping her hands on the grease rag.

"Is there a problem?" he asked, hoping it was nothing serious. He didn't have time for serious. "The car's brand new. There shouldn't be a problem."

Jessie shook her head. "No problem. Not really."

Cameron waited. She avoided eye contact and he had the distinct impression she was stalling for time. What the hell was going on?

He glanced over at Garza. *He* was looking decidedly uncomfortable, too.

"All right," Cameron said. "If something is wrong with my car, I need to know."

Sam stepped between him and Jessie. Like it was his right to protect her. Cameron shoved the feeling of irritation aside.

"Nothing's wrong with your car," Sam said. "I wanted to take the engine apart. I've never had the chance to work on a Jag before."

"*What*?" Cameron shouted.

Jessie stepped from behind Sam. "It was *me*, Cameron. Not Sam. I was the one who wanted to examine the engine. Sam tried to talk me out of it, but I insisted. It only took five minutes to change the fan belt. You know how much I like engines. I had to have more. I couldn't help myself."

Cameron stared at her and tried to remember his anger, but failed when desire slammed him in the gut.

With chin held high, Jessie's emerald eyes sparkled in defiance. The tails of her shirt were tied beneath her breasts. Every breath she drew, every rise and fall of her chest, hinted of nipple straining against thin cloth.

Her Levi's molded her slim figure, so tight Cameron felt himself harden. He wanted to trace the seams with his finger, or better yet, his tongue, starting from the slender waist, down the flat belly, to the apex between Jessie's thighs.

Hold on, McCade. Slow down.

Jessie watched Cameron boldly inspect her from head to toe. Her nipples tightened as his gaze lingered on her breasts. Her breath hitched when it stalled below her waist. Why in the world hadn't she worn her coveralls today? A shimmering wave of heat spread downward as those blue eyes made sweet love to her.

She felt a rush of dampness on her panties as her body reacted instinctively. Jessie glanced at the hard bulge behind the zipper of Cameron's jeans. Her throat went dry and her stomach lurched uncontrollably.

Why in heaven's name was she so attracted to this man? She had been married and knew all about sex. Her loins ached as a familiar warmth blossomed inside. It had been a long time since TR had died. A long time since she had lain beneath a man. The unbidden picture formed in her mind of Cameron rising above her. Good lord, what was she thinking?

Cameron jammed his hands in his pockets and surveyed the engine parts strewn across the floor. "Can you put it back together?"

Jessie lifted her chin higher at the taunt. "Of course, I can put it back together," she said. "And don't worry, there's no extra charge." She turned to pick up a wrench and felt strong fingers clamp around her upper arm. Cameron pulled her to face him. Was he angry at her sarcasm? *He* was the one who had started it. He knew damn well she could put an engine together blindfolded.

Sam stepped closer and tension flared between the two men with Jessie caught in the middle. She wriggled free from Cameron's hold and turned to Sam. "Let's take a break. It's almost noon. We'll finish after we eat. Unless you're in a hurry?" she said to Cameron over her shoulder. Not waiting for a response, she raced toward the office.

Would Cameron follow her? Did she want him to?

Damn, Jess. Get it together, girl.

Once inside the office, she barricaded herself behind the desk and watched Cameron's approach through the glass door. The bell jingled when it closed behind him. He didn't say anything for a minute, just stood there looking at her. Jessie straightened a stack of papers on her desk. The sensual current flowing between them disturbed her in more ways than the obvious. She had never felt anything like it before. Okay, she was lying. She'd felt it before, but only with Cameron.

Clearing her throat, she kept her focus on the desktop. "I'm sorry about the Jaguar. That was very unprofessional of me. I'll have it ready later this afternoon. No charge."

Cameron walked closer to the desk. "That's not very professional, either. You have to make a living."

Jessie shrugged. "Yes, well..."

"I'll pay for the fan belt." He looked around the office. "Nothing's changed much since the last time I was in here. Do you remember?" His voice sounded like melted chocolate, seeping into every pore of her body.

"The night of the prom," she said softly. He'd looked so handsome in his black tux and baby-blue shirt. They had been kids, but the attraction had been strong. It was stronger now, more irresistible, and much more dangerous.

Cameron nodded. "I remember you pinning my boutonniere on my tux. It took several tries before you got it right."

"Because my hands were trembling."

"You were very young–"

"And scared."

"I didn't mean to scare you, Jess. I remember how nice you looked in that dress."

"Quite a change from the coveralls." She'd been so proud of that beautiful dress and so nervous wearing it.

"Oh yeah, quite a change." He smiled and his eyes lasered in on her. "Have lunch with me, Jess."

That jerked her away from the faraway memories. "What?"

"Let me take you to lunch. For old time's sake."

Jessie shook her head. Not a good idea. "I always go home for lunch."

Cameron stepped around the desk and into her space. "Then how about dinner, tonight?"

She backed away, stopping only when the tall metal file cabinet bit into her shoulder blade. "I don't think so."

Cameron moved closer and stood directly in front of her. His musky male scent invaded her senses. She couldn't stop herself from inhaling deeply, filling her lungs with him.

"Come on, Jess. For old time's sake, let me take you to dinner," Cameron said. "Does the cafe still serve its famous chicken-fried steak?" He grinned boyishly and Jessie's heart turned over.

She smiled back. "Of course, and Sarah Sue still makes the best chocolate cake in the whole state of Texas."

He closed his eyes and sighed. "Oh yeah, Sarah Sue's homemade cakes. Makes my mouth water just thinking about them." Opening his eyes, he put his hands on her shoulders, grasping them lightly. "Let me take you tonight, Jess. Please?"

She swallowed again, wondering if the subtle nuance was deliberate. The frightening thing was that Jessie *wanted* him to take her and not just to dinner.

Why not go with him? She was a grown woman, a widow, for crying out loud. She could handle the attraction and the temptation. She'd have to be careful, that's all. Besides, a chance to go out with Cameron might never come again.

"All right," she said. "I'll meet you at the cafe around six."

"I'll pick you up."

"No, I'd rather meet you there." Jessie knew she was throwing caution to the winds. She also knew she wasn't ready to be alone with him at her house. Or anywhere, for that matter.

Her tummy dropped to her toes when he leaned down to look her square in the eye. "Okay, I'll meet you at the cafe. But next time, I'm picking you up."

Next time?

His breath whispered against her lips. A liquid warmth spread through her veins as his hands slowly moved over her shoulders and neck. He traced her jaw with a gentle finger, rubbed her lips with his thumb. His touch was magic, sending thrills and chills along her nerve endings.

Was he going to kiss her? Did she want him to?

The loud ringing of the telephone shattered the moment. Jessie couldn't decide whether to answer it or jerk the old contraption from the wall. Cameron stepped away, and she had no choice but to pick up the receiver.

"Kincaid's Garage." Her voice quivered. Cameron may have backed off, but his eyes were slowly devouring her. Jessie felt a warm blush spread the entire length of her body.

"Hello, Mrs. Perkins." She concentrated on the little old woman on the other end of the line. "Yes, this afternoon will be fine. Go ahead and bring your car in. It shouldn't take long to fix. Bye, now." She hung up and jotted a note for Sam.

Cameron slipped the pencil from her fingers and dropped it on the desk. He pulled her into his arms, flush against his hard body. Jessie's breasts tingled from the contact of his muscled chest. He removed her baseball cap and smoothed her hair back from her temple. "Remember Lover's Point, Jess?"

The rugged intimacy of his voice almost made her heart stop. She searched the hard planes of his face. "I remember. I didn't think you did though."

"Oh yeah, I remember. I want to kiss you again," he said softly. "Do you want me to kiss you?"

Jessie licked her lips and nodded.

With both hands tenderly cradling her head, Cameron tilted her face up and lowered his mouth until his lips hovered over hers.

Jessie closed her eyes. Yes, she wanted him to kiss her; she *needed* him to kiss her. Would her memories live up to the reality? When the office door opened and the bell jingled, she swallowed a groan of frustration and pushed out of the embrace.

Sam stood on the threshold. "I thought you had already gone to lunch."

"I was just about to leave." She grabbed her cap and jammed it on her head, striving to get hold of her emotions. "I'll see you tonight, Cameron. Six o'clock."

He exchanged a territorial-male-kind-of-look with Sam, then stared down at her. The passion in his gaze left Jessie breathless. He brushed the back of his hand gently against her cheek. "Don't be late. I hate to be kept waiting."

Cameron pushed past Sam and stalked out the door. Goosebumps flittered across the surface of Jessie's skin. What in the world had she gotten herself into?

The afternoon passed quickly. Jessie put the engine back in the Jaguar while Sam worked on Mrs. Perkins' sedan. When she finished with the Jag, she sat in her office in front of her computer for a couple of hours and crunched the numbers again for the thousandth time.

Soon, she'd have to make a tough decision that

would probably cost her friendship with Ruth McCade.

Jessie had promised her friend she'd never lease the mineral rights on the portion of the Diamondback Ranch she'd inherited from TR. But where else could she get the money she so desperately needed? It was either break her promise or lose the garage. What choice did she have?

At a quarter to five, she left the garage and rushed home to get ready for her "date." In the two years since TR's death, she could count the times she'd been out with a man on one hand with fingers left over. Not much experience in that department, even when she was younger. Especially when she was younger.

She pulled the truck around back of the house and parked. Gazing at the home she and TR had shared together, Jessie drew in a deep breath. It couldn't compare to the magnificence of the Diamondback ranch house, but it had a charm all its own. She loved this place; she loved living in a real house. Before marrying TR, she had lived with her father in the tiny rooms behind the garage. If only she could have loved TR like he deserved.

Loud barks greeted her when she climbed out of the pickup. "Down, Sherlock! Down, boy." The German shepherd followed her to the door where a large orange tabby waited, meowing impatiently. "I know, Katnip, I know. Life's tough for an old tomcat."

Jessie opened the door and switched on the lights. The animals bounded past her into the kitchen. After feeding them, she stood at the sink and thoroughly washed her hands with a degreaser until all traces of black disappeared.

She enjoyed working at the garage. Really, she did. But seeing Cameron again had resurrected the dreams of her youth. Her life was satisfying, she reminded herself. Comfortable. Rewarding. Only sometimes a little lonely.

Jessie quickly showered and changed into a cream-colored sweater and dark brown slacks. Sitting at her vanity, she applied mascara and a dab of lipstick, then frowned at her reflection in the mirror.

She really shouldn't be going out with Cameron McCade. TR had hated the McCades with a passion. There'd been a feud of some sort between his grandfather and theirs. Jessie had never found out what it was all about. But she did know it had something to do with the mineral rights. The same ones she was going to be forced to lease in order to raise money to save the garage.

She hadn't allowed TR's feelings to interfere with her friendship with Ruth McCade. And she wouldn't let her husband's animosity toward the McCades stop her from going out just this once with Cameron. She had many regrets concerning her marriage to TR Devine. One more added to the pile wouldn't matter that much.

Jessie grabbed her purse and let herself out of the house. She'd always had a weakness for Cameron McCade. That had never changed and probably never would.

CHAPTER THREE

*I*nside Sarah Sue's Cafe, almost all the tables and booths were occupied. It seemed everyone in town was here tonight. Delicious scents of fried chicken, meatloaf and fresh-baked bread wafted in the air. Cameron looked around, spotted an empty booth and made his way across the crowded room. Old friends and neighbors greeted him from all sides. He stopped several times to exchange howdy-dos and good-to-see-yous. So much for the quiet intimate dinner he'd planned.

As soon as he sat down, the door opened and in walked Jessie. Damn, she looked good. The sweater she wore hugged her pretty breasts and her feminine curves filled the tight slacks. Desire riveted through his body. He was starving for a taste of her. Later, he promised himself. Dinner first, kisses later.

She didn't see him at first as she scanned the room, so he stood and waved. She smiled and nodded and started weaving her way around the tables. Of course, she had to pause every few feet and say hello to people. When he couldn't stand the wait any longer, Cameron moved toward her. Ignoring the raised eyebrows and knowing smiles, he grasped Jessie's elbow and practically dragged her from the Johnson's table, where she stood conversing.

"What do you think you're doing?" she said in a furious whisper.

Cameron helped her into the booth and slid in on the opposite side. "You're having dinner with me, not half the town."

Jessie narrowed her eyes and sat back, crossing her arms over her chest. "I've known these people all my life. And so have you, if you bothered to look around."

"I already looked around and said my hellos, while I was waiting for you."

"So you haven't completely forgotten the friendship and fellowship of living in a small town," she said.

"No, I haven't forgotten–"

He fell silent when a tall woman with gray hair rushed up to the table, carrying menus and two glasses of ice water.

"Evenin', Jessie. I'm running late. Just got here and we're short staffed tonight." Sarah Sue handed her a menu then turned to Cameron and nearly spilled the water when recognition dawned. "Good lord! If it isn't Cameron McCade! How you doing, darlin'?"

She set his water and menu on the table and bent down to hug him. "It's right nice to see you again. You haven't been in my café in a coon's age."

"It has been a while. I'm very glad to be back." He shot a challenging look at Jessie. She just smiled at him over her menu.

Sarah Sue patted his cheek, just as if he were fifteen years old, instead of thirty-five. "You always were a handsome boy. Broke all the girls' hearts when you left Salt Fork. You here for Ruth's birthday?"

"Wouldn't miss it for the world."

"Well, I'm sure Ruth is mighty glad you're home. Y'all ready to order, or do you need a minute?"

"I think we're ready. Here, I don't need the menu." Cameron handed it back to Sarah Sue. "I know exactly what we want... give us two orders of chicken-fried steak and two pieces of chocolate cake. That okay with you, Jess?"

Jessie nodded and closed her menu.

Sarah Sue grabbed a yellow pencil from behind her ear and jotted down the order. She stood a moment, looking from Jessie to Cameron, then winked before heading to the kitchen.

Shaking her head, Jessie's cheeks turned pink as she squeezed the lemon slice into her water, then took a sip.

"You're beautiful when you blush," Cameron said. "I want to kiss you again. I want to do a lot more than just kiss you."

Jessie nearly choked on her ice water. With a trembling hand, she set the glass down, sloshing water onto the table. Grabbing a napkin, she dabbed haphazardly at the droplets, her face rosier than ever.

"Here, let me help." He reached over and used his napkin to sop up the puddle. His hand brushed against hers, and he frowned when Jessie jerked back as if she'd touched a live coal.

Cameron folded his napkin. Had he shocked her? It wasn't like when they were kids and she'd been untouched. He gripped the napkin tightly in his hand, wishing he could have been the one to touch her first. Jessie had always been special. He had wanted her that night on Lovers' Point. He ached from wanting her now.

"Relax, Jess. I'm not going to do anything you're not comfortable with. But I won't lie to you, either. There's something between you and me. It was there the night of the prom. It's here between us now."

"I know," she said. "But you're moving too fast for me. Let's take it slow and easy." She tried to smile.

"I'll do my best, sweetheart. That's all I can promise." Not for a moment did he think it would be slow and easy when they came together. It would be hard and fast. He adjusted his position on the vinyl seat of the booth, hoping like hell he could keep his promise.

Sarah Sue waltzed up to the table, carrying a loaded tray. She placed the plates in front of them. "Careful, they're hot. Anything else you need?"

"I don't think so," Cameron said. "Thanks."

Sarah Sue tucked the tray under her arm. "I'm glad you're back, Cameron McCade. And I'm so glad you brought Jessie to dinner. The poor darlin' doesn't get out near enough. Y'all enjoy."

Jessie groaned and Cameron smiled at the murderous look she shot at Sarah Sue's retreating back.

"Maybe you have the right idea about not living in a small town," she said. "I'd give anything to be in a large, impersonal restaurant right now."

"Oh, I don't know. I'm kind of enjoying the fellowship." He grinned, then took a bite of his steak.

Jessie smiled back. "Do I detect a change of heart?"

Cameron shrugged. "I can think of a couple of things I like about small towns. *This* town in particular."

"Such as?"

"Sarah Sue's chicken-fried steak," he said. "And a certain female mechanic, who took apart my brand new car when nothing was wrong with it."

Cameron watched the chin lift and the green eyes sparkle with mischief. His body instantly responded. It took an enormous effort not to lean over and kiss those moist lips.

Then Jessie smiled at him again–a secret smile, an intimate smile–before turning her attention to her dinner. Cameron's gut clenched with desire. He hadn't been this hot for a woman in years. Seventeen years, to be exact.

Jessie watched Cameron sigh with pleasure and push away his empty dessert plate. When he wiped his mouth with his napkin, her heart did a little skip. She wanted to feel that mouth on hers.

All during dinner, she'd been hyper-aware of the man sitting across from her. Their legs had brushed several times beneath the table, each encounter shooting sensual shock waves through her body. She felt on edge with expectancy. Like something important was about to happen.

Unlike Cameron, Jessie didn't believe in plans. In her experience, life was a crapshoot and the luck of the draw; life dealt you a hand of cards, and you made the best of it. Or not. No use planning anything, because something would invariably come along to upset all your careful arrangements.

Sarah Sue walked up to the table holding a steaming coffee pot. "Y'all want more coffee?"

Cameron nodded. "That would be great. How about you, Jess?"

"Yes, please."

After Sarah Sue filled their cups, Cameron settled back against the cushioned booth. "So, tell me about this clinic of yours."

"It's not *my* clinic," Jessie said.

"Well, that's what Mom calls it. She always refers to it as *Jessie's clinic*."

Jessie smiled. "That sounds like something Ruth would say."

"Yeah, Mom gets an idea in her head and it's hard to budge her from it. So, how'd you get on the bandwagon? Why is a medical clinic so important to you? No one's ever wanted to build one in Salt Fork that I've known about. Everyone's been content with the hospitals in Abilene and Lubbock."

"Seemingly content," Jessie said. "When Dad was diagnosed with cancer, it would have been so much easier if we'd had a resident physician in town."

"A country doctor couldn't treat cancer, Jess."

"I know that, but he or she could have treated him for pain and some of the other side effects. Instead, we were always having to pack up and go to Abilene for every little thing."

"I see your point. Eighty miles is a long way to travel to see a doctor."

"And that's just one way. Then there was TR's accident," Jessie continued. "If we'd had a clinic in Salt Fork, with a doctor and oxygen, maybe he could have been saved. As it was, the drive to Abilene just made his injuries worse. He was in a coma for two months. It was awful."

"You must have loved him very much."

"He was my husband. It was hard to see him die."

"I'm sure it was," Cameron said. "Life's dealt you some pretty hard blows: Your mom, your dad, your husband. I really admire how you've bounced back and moved on with your life."

Oh, if that were only true. Jessie shrugged. "I haven't had much of a choice. I've just rolled with the punches."

"So, when can I see this clinic of yours? You've got me curious about it."

"How about tomorrow? No, wait, not tomorrow. I have to go to Lubbock."

"Lubbock?"

"I have some business to take care of. How about the day after tomorrow? I can take a long lunch and show you around."

"Sounds good, Jess. Where is it, by the way? I didn't see it on the main drag."

"It's over on Elm Street, by the high school. Why don't you meet me there around twelve-thirty?"

"I'll pick you up. I *will* have my car back by then, won't I?" he said with a teasing lilt to his voice.

"Of course," Jessie said with a smile. "You could have picked it up this afternoon."

"I could have picked it up this morning, if the engine hadn't been scattered all over the floor." He winked and her tummy fluttered in response.

"I told you I was sorry about that."

Cameron leaned toward her over the table. "Hey, I was kidding. I think it's great you're so enthusiastic about your work."

"And you're not?"

Cameron sat back, exhaling a long breath. "I used to be. Not lately, though."

"Why is that?" Jessie asked. "What happened? From what Ruth's told me, all of your plans have worked out so far. And now you're up for a dream promotion. All should be right with your world."

"You'd think so. I thought moving away from the ranch would cure my restlessness, but it didn't."

He stirred his coffee and placed the spoon on a paper napkin. "For so long, I thought I knew exactly what I wanted. But lately, I feel like all my plans were wasted. I still don't know what the hell I want. I shouldn't be telling you this. You've had enough to deal with and don't need to hear me whine."

Without thinking, Jessie reached across the table and placed her hand over his. "Sometimes, talking helps you see things in a different light. I'd like to think we could be friends, Cameron."

He reversed positions of their hands, with him

holding hers in a tight clasp. His sapphire-blue eyes suddenly glittered hotly. The intensity in Cameron's eyes would be her downfall, she was certain of it.

"I'd like to think we could be more than friends," he said, squeezing her hand. "In fact, I think we're already more than friends."

That bubble of expectancy grew in Jessie's stomach. She tried to retrieve her hand, but he wouldn't let her. "I've never been good with the male/female thing," she said.

He grinned at her, showing that tantalizing hint of dimple. Jessie braced her feet on the floor so she wouldn't slither under the table into a puddle of mush.

"If I remember correctly, you were quite good at the male/female thing. Up on Lover's Point, even though it was your first kiss, you learned very quickly. Oh God, Jess, you don't know how close I came to changing my plans after kissing you."

Jessie pulled her hand back, and this time he let go. "Obviously, I wasn't that good. I never saw you again except when you stopped by the garage for gas on your visits to the ranch."

"You were too young," he said. "*I* was too young. I had to go with my plans, Jess. I never wanted to be a rancher or farmer like my father and brothers. I always wanted to be a doctor."

"I know, Cameron. I understood, even back then."

"I'd like to see you while I'm here," he said. "Let's explore this thing between us, find out where it takes us."

She took a deep breath and nodded, wondering how

and where it would end and whether she would survive this time around. "Okay. Sure, I'd like that, too."

Cameron and Jessie walked out of the café and into the clear cool night. Millions of stars twinkled brightly in the velvety black West Texas sky. The breeze whipped Jessie's hair across her face. Before he could help himself, Cameron brushed the tendrils back over her forehead. Her skin was smooth and warm, her hair like satin. He needed to pull her against him, right here, right now. He didn't care who the hell saw them. He was dying a thousand deaths from wanting, needing to taste her.

Jessie froze under his touch. Her eyes held a wary expression, plus something else. A latent passion, an awareness of the crackling energy flowing between them. It had been there all during dinner.

Cameron nudged her forward, away from the cafe's neon light. He splayed his hand on the small of her back and kept it there, not letting it slide down the curve of her sexy bottom like he was itching to do.

"Where are you parked?" he asked, his voice harsh with desire.

"Way in back."

Frowning, Cameron guided her along the side of the cafe. "Don't you know it's not safe to park behind buildings?"

She looked up from digging in her purse for her keys. "Not safe? What could possibly happen?"

"You could be mugged or worse."

"Don't be silly. This is Salt Fork, not Houston," she said with a smile. "No one's ever gotten mugged around here."

He held out his hand. "Give me your keys. I'll open the door for you."

"Boy, you have been gone a long time," she said. "Nobody locks their car, even in town. Remember?"

Muttering under his breath, he started to open the truck door, then changed his mind. He wrapped his fingers around her arm and pulled her against him. She dropped her purse and stared at him, then his lips.

"Unlocked doors. Parking in the back. It could be very easy for someone to grab you," he said. There was no fear in Jessie's eyes, only awareness.

Cameron gripped her bottom and cradled her body into his. She fit perfectly, smelled wonderful. He forgot all about taking things slowly. Her mouth was too close, too inviting.

He intended to have just one quick taste as he lowered his mouth to hers. Jessie melted into his embrace. When she sighed a sexy little sigh, something snapped inside of him. He pushed her against the truck, his hard thighs pressing into her softness. He clasped both sides of her head and slanted his mouth, plunging his tongue deeply into her sweet warmth. His fingers slid into her silky hair as he trailed hot kisses along her cheekbone and down her neck.

Jessie tilted her head and arched her body. Cameron felt her hands digging into his shoulders, as if hanging on for dear life. A soft whimper in the back of her throat fueled the desire raging in his veins. He took her mouth again, cupping her breast in the palm of his hand. Blood pounded in his temples and his groin. He couldn't get enough of her.

Jessie's body was on fire. Every nerve ending screamed for more of Cameron's touch. His lips burned a path wherever they roamed. She pulled him closer and felt his hardness pushing against her stomach.

Standing on tiptoe, she instinctively rubbed against him, seeking to ease the raw emptiness inside. Skimming her fingers over the powerful shoulders and neck, Jessie felt the corded muscles bunch up and the tendons grow taut. The coiled tension in his big body begged for release; her own body pleaded for more.

He sought her mouth once again, his tongue thrusting inside, his thumb brushing her nipple. Pressing closer, Cameron covered the length of her body with his. Every stroke of his tongue, every touch of his thumb carried Jessie higher into a maelstrom of sensation, building to such a crescendo she thought she might die from the scorching pleasure.

Cameron tightened his hold on her. The soft warmth of her skin beckoned to him from beneath the woolly sweater. "I *need* you, Jess. I'm burning up for you. Let me follow you home."

"I don't think that's a good idea," she managed to say.

He searched her face. "Why not?"

"This is happening too fast. I thought we agreed to take it slow and easy. Besides, I'm not ready." She shrugged away and turned to open the truck door.

He couldn't let her go. Not yet. He pinned her against the truck again, supporting himself with his hands on either side of her, pressing his body against the supple curves of her back and bottom. "You're ready," he breathed in her ear. "You want me as much as I want you. Don't deny it, Jess. We'd be good together and you know it."

She closed her eyes, leaning her forehead against the glass of the window. His voice was low and seductive. Jessie felt delicious shivers skitter over her skin where his body touched hers from behind. Cameron nuzzled her ear lobe, his strong hands reaching around to caress her breasts. She desperately wanted to give in to the desire surging between them. It would be so easy to invite him home. But afterwards? There would be no afterwards. He was returning to Houston, and she was staying in Salt Fork.

Jessie turned around. Before she could explain, Cameron swept her into his arms again, crushing her mouth with a deep hot kiss. All logical reasons to deny him disappeared as physical sensation took over, carrying her on the waves of desire.

Loud voices and the thud of heavy boots brought Jessie crashing down to earth. She placed her hands on Cameron's chest and pushed with all her might.

"Damn." He gave her one more quick kiss before stepping away.

Jessie hurriedly smoothed her hair into place and held her breath, hoping that whoever it was would just get in their car and drive away. She wasn't so lucky.

"Hey, Jessie. Is that you? You all right?"

Picking up her purse, she straightened. Parker Hendricks and Jason Turner stood by their trucks, craning their necks to see who she was with. "Yes, Parker. I'm okay."

"Who you got with you?" The two lanky cowboys strolled over. Their eyes widened and two grins split their suntanned faces. "Well, I'll be damned," Parker said. "How you doin', McCade? Been a long time, ain't it?"

"Too damned long." Cameron shook both their hands.

"Visiting the old home place, are you?" Jason asked. "Shouldn't forget all your old friends here in Salt Fork, just 'cause you live the good life in Houston."

"I'm beginning to think you're right," Cameron said.

"What are you boys up to?" Jessie asked, her heart still racing. She glanced at Cameron. He was breathing hard and his dark eyes still blazed with hunger.

Jason shrugged. "We were just gonna grab a bite to eat, then get on back to the ranch. Working at the C&L, you know."

Parker frowned at Jessie. "Did you and Cameron eat dinner together? Are y'all on a *date*?"

Jessie cringed inwardly. Already, speculation would be running rampant in town. People would talk, and when Cameron left, everyone would look at her and feel sorry for her. "We didn't come together," she said.

"She wouldn't let me pick her up," Cameron told them. "And she won't let me see her home."

Jessie frowned at him. Cameron seemed to be enjoying her predicament.

"Aw, Jess," Parker said. "How many times have people told you to go out and have some fun? Cain't bury yourself, just because old TR passed on to his reward. You're young, girl. Let McCade see you home." He winked at her and smiled at Cameron. Jason nodded in agreement.

Jessie wanted to bash their heads together. Cameron stood there waiting, challenge gleaming in his blue eyes. He'd quickly turned this interruption to his advantage. What had happened to his promise to go slowly?

"We came in separate cars," Jessie said. "I wouldn't want Cameron to go out of his way."

"Hell, your place is right on the way to the Diamondback Ranch. You let McCade see you home." Parker turned to Cameron. "How's old Dallas doing, anyway? Ain't seen him in a couple of weeks."

"Everyone's fine," Cameron said. He opened the truck door for Jessie, ignoring the murderous look in her eyes. "Thanks for your help, fellas. I'll follow Jessie home now. Nice seeing you both."

"Anytime, McCade. Don't be a stranger, you hear? Take care, Jess." Parker slapped Cameron on the back and winked again.

Jessie started the engine and threw the truck into reverse. She had no intention of waiting for Cameron. Maybe he'd change his mind and go home. He'd *better* change his mind, because she wasn't going to let him in her house tonight. If he couldn't slow things down, then she would have to do it. Putting the truck into drive, she left the three men standing in the parking lot staring after her.

Parker pushed back his Stetson and shook his head. "What made Jessie so mad? She sure left in a hurry."

"You going after her?" Jason asked Cameron.

"No, I don't think so," he said. "See you around, Parker. Jason. It's time for me to head on back to the ranch anyway. Good night." Cameron turned and walked toward Dallas's truck.

How could he have lost control like that when he'd kissed Jessie? He was the master of control. But standing with her alone under the bright stars–he hadn't been able to resist temptation. Damn, she'd felt good in his arms and she'd tasted hot and sweet.

Cameron looked down the road at the rapidly vanishing taillights of Jessie's truck. That was the second time she had fled from him. Like she was running scared. That was not what he wanted. Not what he wanted at all.

CHAPTER FOUR

*I*t was late afternoon the next day before Cameron picked up his car from the garage. He and Dallas had gone to Abilene to buy their mom's birthday present. Dallas dropped him off at Kincaid's on the way back to the ranch.

A quick look in the empty garage sent Cameron to the small office. Fire kindled his blood at the thought of seeing Jessie again. The bell on the door tinkled a friendly greeting, but Cameron didn't feel the least bit friendly when he saw Sam Garza sitting behind the old oak desk.

The glass door swished closed behind him as he glared at Garza. "Where's Jessie?"

Sam didn't look up from the receipts he was sorting. "She had business in Lubbock this morning. Then she called and said she wouldn't be in today."

Cameron stepped forward. The man acted like he

owned the place. What kind of relationship did Garza share with Jessie, anyway?

"Is something the matter with her? Is she sick?" He kept his voice calm, putting a lid on his rising hostility. If he didn't know better, he'd say he was jealous, which was ridiculous. Wasn't it?

Sam tilted back his chair and clasped his hands behind his head. "I don't know what's wrong with her. This is the first time she's missed work since I've been here. Maybe she doesn't want to see you again." Righting the chair, he rose slowly to his feet, leaning his fists on the desk. "I think she's scared of you."

"There's no reason for Jessie to be afraid of me."

"I think she has a very good reason," Sam said. "She's afraid she'll get hurt. I wouldn't want that to happen, you understand?"

Cameron understood all right. "Are you in love with Jessie?"

Sam threw back his head and laughed. Cameron didn't know whether the man was laughing in amusement or bitterness.

"Who wouldn't love Jessie once they know her? She's beautiful and smart. And a damned good mechanic." Sam shrugged his shoulders. "When I came to Salt Fork, her husband had recently died. She was advertising for someone to help in the garage. I applied for the job and I've been here ever since. I love Jessie, but I'm not *in love* with her."

"So, you're her self-appointed guardian?"

Sam shrugged again. "She has no one else."

Cameron leaned forward and stared hard at Garza.

The man didn't flinch or back away. "Let me make one thing perfectly clear. I don't intend to hurt Jessie in any way. She's a grown woman and can make her own decisions. Now, how much do I owe for the car?"

He pulled out his wallet and waited. Garza looked like he wanted to say something more, but didn't. He quickly flipped through the day's receipts and handed Cameron his bill.

Jessie scattered seed for the chickens, then gathered the eggs, placing them gently in her wicker basket. She replenished their water before herding the matronly brood into the henhouse for the night. After locking the door against nightly marauders, she headed for the house with Sherlock and Katnip following closely at her heels.

Dusk cloaked the barnyard as night settled in; the lone evening star twinkled in the sky. Crickets chirped their night song, and a soft breeze rustled the last of the leaves on the big oak tree near the back door. As the sun gave up its last vestiges of light, the halogen lamp on the tall pole in front of the house flickered on, casting a comforting glow around the yard.

Jessie stopped a moment under the lamp pole and breathed in a deep lungful of fresh air, enjoying the night sounds all around. What a stressful day it had been. In Lubbock, she'd seen her lawyer and set the groundwork to lease the oil rights she owned on the Diamondback Ranch. She hadn't actually committed the vile deed yet, but everything was in place. One phone call to Mr.

Bennett, and he'd put the wheels in motion and make it happen.

Jessie kept hoping against hope that a miracle would occur–maybe she'd win the lottery or something, so she wouldn't have to make that call. But in reality, there were no other options available. Jessie knew she was going to be forced to renege on the promise she'd made to Ruth McCade. She didn't see any other way to get the money she desperately needed. She would have to warn Ruth; she owed her that much.

Jessie spotted the headlights of a car through the grove of mesquite trees bordering the dirt road leading to the house. Sherlock took exception to the newcomer and dashed to the edge of the lawn, barking loudly.

When the black Jaguar pulled up, Jessie's heart plummeted. She'd purposely stayed away from the shop today because she'd wanted to avoid another meeting with Cameron. She had tried not to think of the night before and that incredible kiss behind the cafe, but her traitorous body wouldn't let her forget. Her breasts ached and the feeling of emptiness deep inside reminded her of her lonely state.

Setting the basket of eggs beside the door, she gathered her courage and waited. And waited. Cameron made no move to get out of the car. Sherlock stood at the door on the driver's side, growling ferociously, his sharp teeth gleaming in the lamplight. For a split second, Jessie had a good mind to go in the house and leave Cameron to his fate. But that was the coward's way out and she wasn't a coward. She'd have to face him sooner or later. With a deep breath for courage, she called

Sherlock to heel. The big German shepherd barked a few more times before relinquishing his position.

Slowly opening the door, Cameron eased out of the sports car. "That's some guard dog you've got there."

Jessie patted Sherlock, who had taken a defensive stand by her side. "He keeps unwanted visitors away."

Cameron squatted on his haunches in front of Jessie and spoke to Sherlock in a soothing voice, allowing the dog to sniff his hand, finally petting him on the scruff of the neck. "Am I an unwanted visitor, Jess?"

Oh no. She wanted him and that was the problem in a nutshell.

"Well, it depends on your intentions," she said. "You come waltzing into town, after being gone for years, and expect me to fall into bed with you. I can't do it, Cameron. I don't know you very well. We went out exactly one time when we were kids. I can't deny the attraction between us, but that's not enough for me. I need more, and I don't think you're willing to give it."

There. She'd said her piece and unburdened her heart. Now, Cameron would go back to Houston and she'd never see him again. Never feel his arms around her... never lie in bed with him...

Cameron rose to his feet and grasped her by the shoulders. An odd expression played across his handsome face. What was he thinking?

Why couldn't she just invite him in the house and let tomorrow take care of itself? She was good at that—taking one day at a time. But somehow, she didn't think it would work in this situation. Guarding her heart was paramount.

"I didn't come to town to seduce you into bed," he said. "I came home for my mother's birthday."

Jessie's legs trembled. She grabbed hold of his forearms, feeling the strong tendons beneath her sensitive fingers, the roughness of the hair covering his skin.

The pressure on her shoulders increased, as Cameron supported her weight. "I won't lie to you, Jess. You know I want you. I wanted you the night of the prom. I want you now. But you have a valid point. We don't know each other very well."

Dropping his hands to his sides, he backed away. Jessie stifled a moan and locked her knees in place, willing them to keep her upright. *Just ask him in, Jess. Don't think about tomorrow.*

"Cameron?" Her voice sounded strange to her ears; her pulse pounded in her throat. She was about to do something totally against her nature. She couldn't let him walk away forever. Not again.

He raised an eyebrow in question, his eyes dilating with desire. The force of the passion radiating between them hit Jessie like a bowling ball crashing down an alley, laying all the pins flat. Her lungs refused to operate and she gasped for breath. One touch from him and she'd be flat on her back like those pins, and to hell with tomorrow.

Before she could speak, Cameron placed a finger on her lips and shook his head. "No. You're right; we do need to get better acquainted. I want to know you inside and out, backward and forward, from the top of your head to the tips of your toes. And everything in between."

Jessie stood mesmerized by the subtle love words and the light pressure of his finger on her lips. Her body craved contact. She remembered the taste of his mouth and wanted to taste it again. Good grief, the man was lethal.

"I won't be here very long," he said. "Let's go out tomorrow night. No pressure, just go out and have fun. You can catch me up on things here, and I'll tell you about Houston and my practice."

Jessie smiled. "You really do enjoy being a doctor, don't you? You had it all planned out when you were young and you made it happen." She hadn't been part of his plans back then. Last night, he'd said he'd almost changed them because of her. Somehow she didn't really believe him.

"Yes, I love being a doctor," he said. "What about tomorrow night, Jess?"

"Where would we go?" She was stalling for time because she wasn't certain where this would lead, how it would end. He wanted her in bed and she wanted him. But then what? He'd return to Houston, she'd be in Salt Fork... she'd been through it all before.

"How about Billie G's?" he said. "We could have a few beers. Play some pool."

Jessie shook her head. The honky-tonk up on the Caprock was popular, but not one of her favorite places. "I don't drink much, and I've never really liked pool."

"Then how about a movie?" Cameron wanted to spend time with Jessie and not just in bed. The more he saw of her, the more he realized how much he'd missed by leaving all those years ago. He traced his fingers along Jessie's jaw, over her collarbone, down her arm.

She shuddered deliciously beneath his touch. Cameron dropped his hand to his side when she stepped away. He forced himself not to grab her and kiss her till she moaned.

"The closest theater is in Cactus Gap, remember?" Jessie swiped her hair back from her face. Cameron wanted to bury his hands in the silky threads. He wanted to bury himself inside her body.

Taking a deep breath, he tried to concentrate on her words instead of the husky tone of her voice. "Right. Cactus Gap's fifty miles away."

"Afraid your car won't make it that far?" Her green eyes widened as soon as the words left her mouth. She'd set herself up and knew it.

Cameron grinned. "No problem. I'll be with one of the best mechanics in Texas. I'm sure she wouldn't leave me stranded."

Jessie laughed.

"I like it when you laugh." Cameron stepped closer and reached for her, thankful she didn't pull away. "I like kissing you, too. I want to kiss you, Jess. I *need* to kiss you."

The laughter died in Jessie's throat when his lips brushed hers. His words touched something deep inside. The kiss was gentle, very different from the passionate one they'd shared last night. Before she had time to respond, Cameron released her. He searched her eyes as if looking for something.

"Will you go to the movies with me?" he asked

softly.

Jessie couldn't speak, still trying to recover from the kiss. She thought he sounded almost hesitant. Like her answer mattered to him a lot. Finally, she just nodded.

Cameron smiled. "Good. When I see you tomorrow for the tour of your clinic, we'll finalize the plans."

Jessie stood in the lamplight after he drove away. She traced her lips with one finger. The gentle kiss they'd shared had been different, nothing like she'd ever experienced before. Especially with Cameron McCade.

The next morning, Jessie rolled herself on the creeper underneath Mrs. Jones's late model SUV and loosened the oil plug. Placing a pan to catch the oil, she mentally willed the black fluid to drain quickly. It was eleven-thirty and she was starving. She hadn't eaten any breakfast. She'd still been shaken by the gentleness of Cameron's kiss the night before. The man confused the hell out of her.

The oil flow stopped and Jessie quickly changed the filter. Wiping her hands on a grease rag, she rolled herself out from under the vehicle. Before she knew what was happening, she was lifted from the creeper and held in Cameron's strong arms. Amused blue eyes stared down at her from beneath his Stetson, and she was certain she had oil on her cheeks. She tried to wipe it away.

Low laughter rumbled in Cameron's throat. He took the rag in one hand, her chin in the other. "You're just making it worse. Let me do it."

Jessie tried to quiet the tremulous pounding of her heart. The firm pressure from Cameron's fingers on her chin warmed her skin and a delicious heat spread downward. A hunger of a different sort made her lean toward him.

Careful, Jess. She grabbed the rag to finish the job herself and stepped away, forgetting about the creeper on the floor. One minute she was falling; the next, she was safely in Cameron's arms again. He held her tightly against the length of his body. But Jessie knew she wasn't safe at all. In fact, she was in too much danger for her peace of mind.

She pushed out of the embrace and desperately tried to get hold of her wayward emotions. "Thanks for catching me."

"My pleasure," he said with a wink.

Prickles of awareness rose on the nape of her neck at the sound of his low, seductive voice. Jessie bent down, picked up her baseball cap and jammed it on her head. She felt like a clumsy fool. Not only for tripping over the cart, but for her lack of control to Cameron's touch.

The look of raw hunger on his face froze Jessie on the spot. What *was* this thing between them? It grew stronger each time they were together.

Jessie tossed the grease rag in the trash barrel. "I didn't expect to see you for another hour. Has something come up?"

Cameron stuffed his hands in his pockets. Something had definitely come up, but it wouldn't be polite to mention it, especially when he had promised Jessie he wouldn't put pressure on her. "Actually, I couldn't wait any longer to see you again. So, I brought lunch. I thought we could go to the roadside park and have a picnic, before you showed me your clinic."

Jessie melted a little inside. How sweet. "Shouldn't you be spending this time with your family?"

"I rode out with Dallas early this morning to inspect the cattle, then visited with Mom at breakfast. I promise you, she didn't mind at all when I said I wanted to have lunch with you. In fact, she packed a basket for us."

"I hope Ruth isn't getting any ideas." Jessie was trying not to get any ideas either.

Cameron smiled. "Mom's always getting ideas. You know how she is. You *are* hungry, aren't you? I stopped by the cafe. There's two pieces of Sarah Sue's carrot cake for dessert."

Jessie's stomach growled in response and she laughed. "You sure know how to tempt a woman. Let me wash up." She turned on her heel and ran to the office, blushing at her unruly tongue.

Know how to tempt a woman? Good grief, what would she say next? She hadn't missed the flash of heat in Cameron's eyes.

After slipping out of her coveralls and making sure her sweater and slacks were okay, she ran a comb through her hair and grabbed her purse. She scribbled a note for Sam to finish Mrs. Jones's SUV when he came back from his break, which would be any minute now.

Jessie hurried outside. The look of admiration on Cameron's face generated a warm sensation in the pit of her stomach. Since she was an expert at compartmentalizing her troubles, she banished all worries and doubts to the back of her mind and decided to enjoy Cameron's company today.

Cameron waited with arms folded, leaning against his car, watching Jessie's approach. She had exchanged her coveralls for a pair of pants that outlined her shapeliness and a sweater that teased his imagination.

He dug his keys from his pocket, glad to release some of the tension from his tight jeans. Since coming to the ranch, he'd been in a constant state of arousal. That in itself was exciting and new. For the past decade, his schedule had been so tight and hectic, he hadn't had much time to pursue the ladies, no matter what his mother thought. He'd essentially put his libido on hold, but Jessie had certainly awakened it.

She stopped in front of him with a smile on her lips. "Ready?"

Oh yeah. "That didn't take long," he said. On impulse, he held out the keys. "Why don't you drive?"

Jessie's green eyes widened with delight. "You trust me with your Jag?"

"Sure, I trust you." He tossed her the keys and she caught them to her chest, the movement pushing her breasts against the plush fabric of her sweater. Cameron swallowed hard. Quickly, he walked to the driver's side and opened the door. "I trusted you to repair the fan belt, didn't I? And since you're intimately acquainted with the engine, you deserve the chance to drive the car."

"You're never going to let me live that down, are you?"

"Not in this lifetime."

Jessie's eyes crinkled with humor. She climbed in the driver's seat and closed the door.

Cameron slid in on the passenger side and buckled his seat belt. Her impish expression made her look about fifteen again. He felt the old familiar tug toward her combined with something dangerously new.

She hesitated a moment, then inserted the key and the motor roared to life. Jessie let out a sigh of contentment. Throwing a mischievous look his way, she floored the gas pedal and the car zoomed onto the gray pavement heading out of town.

"Better slow down," Cameron said. "You don't want to get a ticket."

"This car wasn't made to go slow." She revved the engine and shot past the city limits.

"I never figured you for a speed demon." He flipped a switch on the console and the roof of the Jaguar folded back. A clear blue West Texas sky appeared above their heads.

Jessie laughed and leaned back against the headrest. "There's a lot you don't know about me."

"I'd like the chance to find out." Cameron watched her in fascination. Her laughter stoked a fire deep within. He had an almost uncontrollable urge to trail kisses along her neck and down her collarbone. When she turned to look at him, inviting him to share her joy, he planted a quick kiss on her smiling lips, pulling away before she had time to respond.

"Cameron!" The car jerked slightly to the right. Immediately, Jessie corrected the angle of the wheels, keeping her concentration on the road.

"Sorry, couldn't resist." He realized he was having a good time and really enjoying himself. No feeling of restlessness, only the pleasant hum of anticipation.

Jessie shook her head, trying to frown, but couldn't. Her hair whipped across her face and her eyes danced with pleasure.

Before long, the roadside park came into view. She pulled up beside the awning-covered tables and handed the keys to Cameron. "Thank you. It was everything I dreamed it would be and more."

Cameron crammed the keys into his pocket, then snagged the picnic basket from the floorboard. Jessie's husky voice, the words she'd spoken, sparked erotic images in his overheated brain. Silently, he counted to ten. *Slow down, McCade.*

Setting the basket on one of the concrete tables, he walked toward the lookout point, where Jessie stood gazing at the view. The park was located on the edge of a deep rocky gorge stretching and twisting as far as the eye could see. Striations of red rock and white gypsum contrasted with the green of mesquite trees and sagebrush. The Double Mountains stood on the horizon, majestic in their height and splendor.

Jessie sighed and held out her hand to Cameron. He hesitated. The gesture invited an intimacy, a closeness he had avoided all his life. He took hold of it gingerly.

She squeezed his hand. "Isn't it beautiful?"

"Breathtaking," he said, staring at Jessie's profile,

admiring the perfection of her features.

Glancing at him, she blushed and tried to remove her hand from his grasp, but he wouldn't let her.

"I meant the gorge and the mountains," she said.

"I'd rather look at you." He lifted her fingers to his lips and kissed each one in turn. Her breath hitched and his body tightened.

She allowed him to finish, before pulling her hands away, dropping them to her sides and knotting them into fists. Clearing her throat, she turned and walked to the picnic table. "What did your mother pack for us? I'm starved." Her voice trembled slightly.

Cameron followed and stood behind her, close enough to feel the heat from her body.

Something about Jessie drew him like a magnet. He didn't want to analyze it; he just wanted to enjoy it. Inhaling her fresh clean fragrance, he touched his lips to her hair. "There's fried chicken, fresh biscuits, and a thermos of hot coffee," he said softly in her ear.

Jessie jerked away and retreated to the other side of the table and lifted her chin. "Look, Cameron. This might be your idea of taking it slow and easy, but it sure isn't mine. Maybe you don't have a problem going to bed with me, knowing we won't be seeing each other again, but I can't do it."

She stood across the table from him, her eyes asking questions he was unable to answer. He knew he felt different about Jessie, but he wasn't ready to explore those differences right now. Seeing her again was having a weird effect on him. The years seemed to have melted away, making him behave like an eighteen-year-old with raging hormones. Ever since he'd pulled into her service station the other night, he'd been acting on raw feelings and impulses.

Definitely not his style. He needed to think things through. Not only about Jessie and what he was feeling for her, but also about what he was going to do about the promotion and his future.

"Jess, I'm sorry–"

"You better take me back to the garage," she said.

"What about the clinic? You said you'd give me a tour. I'd really like to see it."

Jessie stood beside the picnic table, indecision warring inside. She suddenly realized the only thing Cameron felt for her was plain old lust. She'd been fantasizing about forever after, a happy ending to her Cinderella fairy-tale night at the prom, and all he wanted was sex.

So much for old dreams, she thought with a sigh. But he could help make one of her new dreams come true– the Salt Fork Medical Clinic.

She'd never planned anything in so much detail as she had in making the clinic in Salt Fork a reality. There had always been setbacks in most of her plans in the past. She'd been walking on eggshells every step of the way in her attempt to get this clinic up and running.

She stared at Cameron across the table. Could she ignore her attraction for him in order to pick his brains about what was needed for a rural medical clinic?

If she wanted to move on with her life, she really had no choice.

"Jess, I'm sorry I've been coming on too strong," he

said. As always, his deep voice oozed over her, turning her bones to jelly. "Let's start over. Can you forgive me and share this picnic with me? Then, I want to see your clinic. You said you needed my advice about it."

That certainly was true, she thought.

"And I promise to keep my hands to myself."

Jessie sighed, and then nodded slowly. Lifting a leg over the bench, she sat at the concrete table. "All right. We'll start over."

"Okay, then." Cameron removed his Stetson, set it on the table and took a seat across from her. He filled a paper plate with a crispy chicken leg and golden biscuit and handed it to her. Then he poured a steaming cup of coffee from the thermos and set it in front of her.

Jessie bit into the piece of chicken, not really tasting it. Her appetite was gone again. Keeping her head down, she covertly watched Cameron fill a plate for himself. He broke a biscuit in two, popping half into his mouth, chewing slowly, gazing intently at her.

Why did he have to be so handsome? Why was she so attracted to him? Why was her life always so complicated? She didn't need this kind of complication right now. She was hanging on by a thread financially. She certainly didn't need to be hanging emotionally, too.

"Mom told me you're having money troubles."

Jessie swallowed wrong and nearly choked.

"Are you okay?" Cameron asked, a look of concern crossing his face. He shoved her cup closer. "Here, take a drink."

She sipped the coffee and scorched her tongue. Damn, she needed to get her act together. Taking three deep breaths, Jessie looked at Cameron. "Ruth told you I was having money troubles?"

He shrugged and popped the other half of his biscuit into his mouth. "She's worried about you. So is Dallas."

Jessie took another sip of coffee, cautiously this time. "I just *bet* Dallas is worried about me."

"Why do you say that?"

"He hasn't told you?"

Cameron selected another piece of chicken from the picnic basket. "He said you've leased the mineral rights on the Devine place, and that you own a large portion of the mineral rights on the Diamondback Ranch. He's afraid you'll lease them to Copper River Oil Company."

"Did he also tell you that I promised I wouldn't, unless absolutely necessary?" She bit into one of Ruth's homemade biscuits and even though it melted in her mouth, she couldn't enjoy it because her stomach was twisted into knots.

"That's what they're afraid of. If you're so short on cash, you might be forced to lease them."

Jessie took a sip of coffee. What could she say? That was exactly her predicament, and her options were fast running out.

"Jess, you aren't going to lease them, are you?"

Once again, Cameron's smooth voice washed over her, causing tingles along her nerve endings. Why couldn't things be different? Why did she always feel guilty and regretful?

"Jess?"

She took a deep breath. "Ruth's right. If I don't come up with some money, I could lose my garage. I can't let that happen."

"Why don't you sell the mineral rights to Dallas?"

Jessie grabbed a napkin and concentrated on wiping her fingers. "I promised TR I would never sell them." Especially to the McCades, but she couldn't say that.

"Why not? Dallas would pay good money. He doesn't want anyone drilling on the ranch, Jess."

She crushed the napkin in her hand. "I can't sell them. I promised."

"You're stubborn, aren't you?"

Jessie shrugged a shoulder. "A promise is a promise, Cameron. I always keep my promises."

He narrowed his eyes. "You promised my mom you wouldn't lease those rights. Looks like you're going to break that promise."

Jessie swallowed the lump in her throat. "Yes, and it's killing me, all right? I can't lose my dad's garage. I need that money."

"So, you've already signed the papers?"

Could she feel any more miserable? Heaving a sigh, Jessie nodded. "Everything's in place. One phone call, and it's a done deal. I don't want to make that call, but I can't see my way out of this money mess without leasing those mineral rights."

"Have you told my mother?"

"No, not yet. I'll give her fair warning and tell her before it actually goes into effect. Please don't tell Ruth or Dallas any of this. I want to tell them myself. Who knows? Maybe something will turn up, and I won't have to make that phone call."

"That's not likely, though."

Her stomach cratered. "No. I've pretty well used up all my resources."

Cameron continued eating, his eyes focused on her.

What was he thinking? Was he angry with her? All of the McCades, even Cameron, loved the Diamondback Ranch. It was in their blood. Just like Kincaid's Garage was in hers.

Jessie pushed her plate away.

"Not hungry?" Cameron asked.

She shook her head.

"How about the cake?"

"No, thanks. But you go ahead."

"We'll save it for later. Let's clean up here, and then you can show me the clinic."

"You still want to see it?"

He gathered the paper plates and food, throwing everything into the basket. "Yeah, why not?"

"I thought... never mind."

Jessie screwed the top onto the thermos and handed it to him. The fleeting touch of his fingers reignited the undeniable awareness between them. She quickly relinquished her hold.

Cameron stood, picked up the basket and waited for her. With a heavy heart, Jessie rose from the table. Damn, she hated having to break her promise to Ruth. It made her sick thinking about it.

"Jess?"

She shook away the morose thoughts and looked up. Cameron stood very close and the look in his eyes made her breath hitch in her lungs. He touched her cheek gently, tracing her jaw line.

All of a sudden, he froze and dropped his hand, then cleared his throat. "I know you have to do whatever it takes to save your father's garage. Don't worry about Dallas and Mom. They'll eventually come around. Things will work out. They always do, one way or another."

Jessie swallowed back the tears threatening to spill. "Thanks, Cameron."

He grabbed his Stetson and jammed it on his head. "Hey, what are old friends for? Now, let's go see this clinic of yours."

CHAPTER FIVE

Cameron followed Jessie into the new metal building across the street from the high school. The sign out front read *Salt Fork Medical Center.* As soon as he stepped foot inside the door, he had a strange feeling of *this is it.* Calmness settled over him, the likes of which he'd never experienced in his entire life.

Maybe he'd wake up and find himself in his bed in Houston, all of this just a pleasant dream.

"Well, what do you think?" Jessie stood near the reception window, a nervous look in her eye. "I tried to choose colors that were restful and reassuring. When people come in sick and feeling out of sorts, I thought the soft green and cream colors would comfort them."

Cameron nodded. Maybe that was it. Maybe it was the color scheme making him feel calm and relaxed. "Works for me."

Jessie let out a huge breath and smiled. "I know the

chairs aren't fancy and the pine tables are plain, but I did the best I could with the available funds."

"It's perfect, Jess. The waiting room is functional as well as inviting. Not your typical clinic at all. I like it."

When she smiled again, his chest constricted. He wanted to kiss her again. He wanted her, period.

"Good," she said. "Wait till you see the medical equipment. No corners cut in that department, I assure you."

Cameron didn't expect much, but when he saw the X-ray machine, the MRI and the ultrasound units, he was duly impressed. "Nice. You have a great set-up here: State-of-the-art medical technology right at the doctor's fingertips. You do this all yourself?"

"Mostly. I visited several clinics in Abilene and Lubbock to see what they had. Research, you know."

Cameron ran his hand over the MRI unit. "You did well. Very well."

"Thanks. Let me show you the rest."

The industrial grade carpet muted their footsteps as Jessie gave him the tour of the three examination rooms, a small lab to study blood and urine samples, a spacious office for the doctor, a lunchroom and laundry room.

After making the entire circuit, they ended back in the reception area. The dark green Formica counters gleamed brightly. Two brand new computers stood waiting on the desks. A large copy machine was flanked by a wall filled with multicolored files.

"So, what do you think?" Jessie asked.

Cameron ran his hand over the wall files, then turned toward her. "*Wow* is what I say. You have everything but the doctors, nurses and patients. I can't imagine what advice you need from me."

Jessie leaned a hip on the counter and crossed her arms. "Now that you've seen the clinic, I was hoping you could recommend a doctor who might be willing to relocate and practice rural medicine. Or maybe tell me how to go about finding such a doctor. The pay's not great and a lot of the patients will be self-employed and won't have insurance."

Cameron could just imagine the waiting room full of farmers and ranchers, their wives and children, the quiet hum of conversation, the rustle of magazines being read by people waiting their turn to see the doctor.

He could picture the bustle of the staff, taking calls and filling out reports. Nurses weighing in patients and escorting them to the examination rooms.

And surprisingly, Cameron could see himself wearing his white coat with a stethoscope around his neck, listening to patients' hearts and looking in ears and throats. Making quick diagnoses and writing prescriptions. Happily practicing medicine and not worrying about hospital politics. Hell, maybe even having time for a social life.

With Jessie.

"Cameron? Can you recommend anyone?" Her soft voice jerked him from his daydreams.

He exhaled a long breath. "I'll ask around and see if anyone might be interested. Give me a little time." It wouldn't do to tell her he was interested. He wasn't certain he was ready to make such a radical switch in his career. He wasn't certain of a lot of things, lately.

"Thanks," she said with a smile.

After looking around one last time, Cameron followed Jessie out of the building. The brisk wind knocked off his Stetson. He caught it before it tumbled to the ground.

Jessie chuckled as she stood by his car. That familiar heat simmered low in his belly. He was aware of her green eyes on him as he opened the car door. Yeah, he wanted her. But he also wanted something more.

Somewhere along the way and through the years, he'd gotten off track. He'd turned into someone he didn't know. Someone he didn't really like.

Coming back home, seeing Jess again, and touring the clinic made Cameron decide that it was definitely time for a new plan.

The ride back to the garage was a quiet one. The silence in the car hung heavy. Showing Cameron the clinic had reminded Jessie of one of her most secret wishes. At first, she'd wanted the clinic built to assuage some of the guilt she felt about her husband. She'd thought a clinic with a doctor and nurse on staff could help save lives and that would make up for her ruining TR's life.

Okay, maybe she hadn't really ruined his life. But Jess felt she'd taken more from the marriage than her fair share. She'd failed to give TR the children he longed for. And she hadn't loved him as she should have. Building the clinic in his honor was her penance.

But as she got more involved in the plans and details, as she saw the clinic become a reality, Jessie couldn't help wishing that Cameron would come back and be the resident physician in Salt Fork.

Yeah, like that was going to happen.

When they reached the garage, Jessie started to unfasten her seat belt.

Cameron covered her hand. "Jess, about tonight–"

She'd forgotten about their date. She didn't think she could continue seeing Cameron, fighting the attraction, and feeling the guilt. Her heart would break when he left for Houston. Whether or not she gave in to this consuming passion, her heart would surely break.

"I don't think it's a good idea for us to go out tonight." Even though she said the words, her hand trembled beneath his. She slowly removed it from his grasp.

Cameron frowned. "Why? I thought we were starting over?"

"We are... we were... but I think it's best if we don't go out tonight." All she wanted was to crawl in a hole and hide away until the dull ache in her chest subsided.

"Why not? I told you I'd keep my hands to myself. Let's go out as friends. Two old friends, catching up on times past."

Who was he trying to kid? Jessie shook her head. "I can't be 'just friends' with you. The chemistry's too strong. I think it's better if we don't see each other again."

"We have to see each other again," he said.

"No we don't."

"Obviously, you've forgotten about tomorrow."

"Tomorrow?" It was Jessie's turn to frown. Was the man dense? Couldn't he tell when he'd been given the brush off?

"The party," he said. "My mother's birthday?"

Jessie groaned. She'd forgotten all about Ruth's party. Most of the town would be there. She'd have to go. Perhaps she could avoid Cameron in the crowd. She summoned up a smile. "Of course... your mother's party. I wouldn't miss it for the world."

"All right then," he said. "The party starts at four. I'll pick you up at three-thirty."

"I'll drive over myself." Jessie tried again to unbuckle her seatbelt, this time succeeding and freeing herself. Suddenly, she felt her wrist enclosed in a strong grasp. Not so free, after all.

Looking at Cameron's large hand, her thoughts ran wild. She longed to feel that hand skimming the entire length of her body, exploring, touching her, loving her. She longed to give in to the overwhelming chemistry they'd always shared.

But afterwards, she'd only feel worse. He wasn't staying, he was going back to Houston.

She tugged her hand and he tightened his fingers, pulling her toward him. Cameron rubbed the underside of her wrist with his thumb. Tiny rivulets of sensation shot up her arm.

"Why do you keep running from me?" he asked softly.

Jessie licked her parched lips and stared at Cameron's mouth. That was a mistake. She wanted that mouth on her body, too. She jerked her hand away and scrambled out of the car. "Maybe it's not you I'm running from."

Jessie stood near the punch bowl, sipping a fruit-flavored drink. She watched as couples whirled by, dancing the Texas Two-Step to the lively country music blaring from a vintage jukebox. Around the edge of the wooden dance platform, gaily-colored lanterns twinkled brightly. Ruth's birthday party was well underway.

The weather had cooperated for once, the temperature was unusually warm for late October and perfect for an outdoor gathering. Half the town had shown up for the festivities. The Diamondback Ranch was famous for its lavish barbecues and parties.

So far, Jessie had managed to avoid Cameron. All afternoon, he had helped Dallas and Austin oversee the smoking barbecue pits. When he wasn't helping his brothers, he stopped to chat with friends and neighbors. Everyone was glad to see him again.

Throughout the evening, Jessie caught glimpses of Cameron as he interacted with his mother's guests. He hadn't once approached her. But the hungry looks he cast her way every now and then, made her stomach flutter with anticipation and dread. She needed to keep him at arm's length. She owed TR that much. Now that dinner was over, maybe it was time to go home.

Jessie ladled more punch into her cup. She wasn't ready to leave just yet. It had been a long time since she'd been to a party. One more drink, then she would call it a night.

"Hey, Jess, pour me one, will you?" Tori McCade stuck her cup under the ladle Jessie was still holding.

"Sure thing," Jessie said. She'd always liked Cameron's baby sister. Only she wasn't a baby any longer. "Haven't seen you in a while. How's veterinarian school going?"

Tori shrugged and sipped her drink. "It's going. I just wish I could hurry up and graduate. Old Doc Pritchard is ready to retire and he's asked me to take over his veterinarian practice here in Salt Fork."

"That's great."

"Yeah, but I have three more years of school left." Tori set her cup down, leaned her elbows on the table and watched the dancers. "It seems like forever."

"It'll go by quicker than you think."

"So speaks the old wizened one."

Jessie grinned. Tori always teased her about being older. They'd been friends for a long time. "You should listen to your elders."

Tori snorted. "Right."

Jessie tapped her foot in time to the music. The dance floor was packed. She smiled when she saw Austin McCade trying to teach his young daughter to dance. It had been ten years since his wife had died, and the man was still grieving. But he was doing a fine job raising Kelsey alone.

Only he wasn't alone, Jessie thought. He had the support of his family to see him through. He was lucky in that respect.

The McCades were good people. Just look at Dallas dancing with his mother. The big taciturn rancher was actually smiling.

Jessie sighed. Dallas wouldn't be smiling when he found out she was going to lease the mineral rights on the Diamondback Ranch. Ruth wouldn't be smiling either.

Tori suddenly straightened from her crouch over the table and poured herself another drink. "I heard you broke a date with Cameron last night."

Jessie nearly choked on her punch. News sure got around fast. "Did he tell you that?"

"No, Mother told me. But I knew something was up the way he was pacing around the living room after dinner, grouchy as a bear. Why'd you break the date? You were only going to the movies, for crying out loud."

"It's complicated. You know how I've always felt about him." Jessie never could figure out how Tori knew, but she did.

"Exactly. And now's your chance."

"Not much of a chance. He isn't here to stay."

"Did you show him the clinic?"

"Yes."

"And?"

"And nothing."

"Well, damn."

"It was a long shot..."

"Don't give up, okay? I've only been home since yesterday, but I've noticed Cameron is even more restless and unsettled than ever. He must be going through a mid-life crisis."

"Oh right, Tori. He's only thirty-five."

"Okay, a *pre*-mid-life crisis, then."

"Whatever you say–"

"Hey, it could be true. Lots of doctors get burned out at an early age. Or they become dissatisfied with the health care system and all the red tape with the insurance companies."

"And you know this how?"

"I'm in grad school. I know. I'm going to be a doctor, too."

"A veterinarian is a whole different animal."

"Oh, that's good," Tori said.

Jessie shrugged, picked up the ladle again and refilled their cups. "Here, have some more punch."

"Pretty good, isn't it?"

"It has an unusual flavor. I can't quite place it."

Tori laughed. Her blue eyes twinkled mischievously. "I spiked it."

"For heaven's sake, why? There's a bar inside."

"Hey, I thought it would be fun. Some of these people really need to loosen up."

"You're getting too old to play these kinds of pranks."

"I'm not the old one here."

"I'm not old, either." Jessie dissolved into giggles. "No wonder I'm feeling light-headed."

"How many cups have you had?" Tori asked with a smile. "I think you're tipsy.

"Who's tipsy?" Sam Garza walked up to the table.

Tori stopped smiling. She plunked her cup down and turned her shoulder. "I better see if Mother needs me," she said, rushing toward the house.

Jessie looked at Sam, who was staring after Tori. "I can't imagine what's gotten into her. She usually isn't rude."

"It doesn't matter," Sam said. "Do you want to dance?"

She loved to dance, but really she needed to get home. So far, she'd been successful in avoiding Cameron, but her luck wouldn't last forever. One dance, then she'd leave.

Smiling at Sam, she said, "I'd love to."

Sam held her in a firm grasp. He set a fast pace, circling the platform, dancing the Texas Two-Step. Jessie held on with a fierce grip; the punch, as well as the swift turns, made her head spin.

When the music stopped, Jessie's head kept twirling. She stumbled and Sam placed his hands on her shoulders to keep her steady.

"Thanks," she said. "I'll be all right in a minute."

He narrowed his eyes. "Have you been drinking?"

Jessie hiccupped. "Only punch."

"*Only punch?* Are you sure?"

Jessie nodded and laughed. "Tori spiked it."

Sam's lips curved in a reluctant smile. "That little witch."

"A charming little witch, don't you think?"

"Much too charming," he said with a frown.

Jessie felt Sam's fingers dig into her shoulders for just an instant. His dark brown eyes held secrets.

"Thanks for the dance." Jessie backed away, but Sam didn't release her. Another song played on the jukebox. Couples swayed to the slow melody.

"How about one more?" he asked.

Jessie hesitated, then nodded. What the hell? One more dance couldn't hurt, could it?

Sam pulled her closer, but not too close. That's what she liked about Sam. She felt safe with him.

Without conscious thought, Jessie laid her head against his shoulder. She felt him stiffen and looked up, wondering if she'd crossed some invisible barrier. Before she could ask what was wrong, a strong hand encircled her waist, turning her away from Sam.

"I believe this is *my* dance." Cameron's voice sent shivers down Jessie's spine. His intense stare made her swallow hard.

"Maybe the lady doesn't want to dance with you." Sam stood his ground, not relinquishing his hold on Jessie.

The tension crackled between the two men. Cameron's touch kindled dormant fires, and her traitorous body responded instantly. She reminded herself about TR and what she owed him, but TR was gone. Cameron was here. More than anything in the world, Jessie wanted to be held in his arms. One time. *One last time.*

"It's okay, Sam," she said.

He glared at Cameron. "You sure?"

"I'm sure."

Immediately, Cameron swept her away. No words were spoken; none were needed. Cameron's eyes never left Jessie's as he held her close. With every movement of the dance, his muscular legs caressed the length of her thighs. Locking his arm around her shoulders, he grasped the nape of her neck. He caught her hand, interlacing her fingers intimately with his.

Jessie remembered him kissing her fingers, one by one. Had that only been yesterday? Cameron was holding her so tightly, she felt his arousal pressing into her and from the look in his eyes, he knew exactly what he was doing.

After circling the floor twice, he clasped Jessie's head into his shoulder, brushing his lips against her hair. His hot breath scorched the sensitive shell of her ear.

Time rolled back and Jessie remembered another dance with Cameron McCade in a darkened gym on prom night. He'd held her close then, too. And her young body had responded with alarming enthusiasm.

But that innocent dance so long ago couldn't compare to what Jessie was feeling now.

Cameron's heart pounded in time to her own. Nothing existed for Jessie except the powerful arms around her, and the musky scent of the man holding her.

When the song ended, he took her by the elbow and led her away into the night. He was breathing hard, walking fast. Jessie had to run to keep up with him. She tried to free her arm, but Cameron ignored her.

"What are you doing? Where are you taking me?" she whispered furiously, glancing back at the diminishing lights surrounding the dance floor.

"I'm taking you someplace where we can be alone. We *need* to be alone."

Cameron pulled Jessie to the side of the huge implement barn, away from prying eyes. He held her for a moment, hugging her close. "I've wanted to do this all evening."

The savage yearning in his voice flowed over Jessie like a blanket of pure desire. An answering ache in the pit of her stomach begged for fulfillment. Tori's punch clouded all reason. Jessie's body burned for one man; she had always burned for one man. He was here, holding her, wanting her.

Cameron touched her cheek, sliding his fingers into her hair, tangling them in the silky bonds. With infinite gentleness, he brought her lips close to his mouth. She felt his breath mingle with hers. The effects of the punch, combined with the intoxicating nearness of Cameron's body, pushed all thoughts of resistance to the back of Jessie's mind.

When his lips finally sought her mouth, she locked her arms around him and gave herself up to the pleasures of the kiss. This would be all she could have. She would not, could not betray TR's memory. This kiss would have to last her for the rest of her lonely life.

Cameron didn't know why Jessie had changed her mind about resisting him. Right now, he didn't care. All that mattered was that she was arching her back, pressing her soft breasts against his chest, clinging to him and responding deliciously to his kisses. They fit together perfectly. He longed to bury himself in her, feel her warmth surround him. He desperately wanted to lie down with her.

Scooping her up in his arms, he kicked open the barn door. Moonlight shone through the upper windows, revealing the hulky shadows of tractors and trailers. His eyes quickly adjusted to the darkness, and he walked to the back where a mountain of soft cottonseed stood. Carefully, he laid Jessie down and stretched out beside her. He rolled over and covered her body with his. He kissed away her small moan of protest, assaulting her senses with renewed passion.

The fresh smell of cottonseed blending with Jessie's perfume drove Cameron wild. He ravaged her mouth, plunging his tongue deep within, tasting her fully.

She'd worn a long, baby blue dress to the party. The dress had bewitched him all day. There were no buttons in back or front, only snaps on one side, starting from under the arm down to the alluring curve of her hip. All afternoon and throughout the evening, those snaps had tantalized his imagination.

Shifting his weight, Cameron tucked a knee between Jessie's legs. The flowing skirt allowed easy access. She parted her thighs and raised her hips, gently rubbing against his iron hard length. Beads of sweat broke out on Cameron's forehead. He forced himself to slow down and fought for control. Jessie's movements were pushing him close to the edge. He deepened the kiss and explored her sweetness. His hands searched out every secret of her luscious body.

Supporting himself on one elbow, Cameron undid the snaps of the enticing blue dress one by one. He slipped a hand under the loosened fabric and eased the lacy edge of Jessie's bra downward, exposing her breasts to his questing fingertips. He cupped the firm flesh in his palm, relishing the silkiness of her skin. She felt heavy and full. God, he had to see her, taste her. He had to get rid of these clothes.

Jerking the bodice out of the way, he looked his fill.

"Beautiful, Jess. You're beautiful." He trailed kisses along the swell of one rounded breast, circling the rosy nipple, teasing the base with his tongue. Then he gently licked the tip and blew softly over the wet peak.

Jessie writhed beneath him, arching her back, seeking more. She reached for him and pulled his head closer, straining upward. Cameron hesitated only a fraction of a moment before taking her into his mouth, swirling his tongue around and around, sucking the nipple hard. Jessie shook her head from side to side, raising her body toward him. The whimpers in the back of her throat grew stronger and louder. His body flexed in response.

He reached under the full skirt and slipped his hand beneath the elastic band of Jessie's panties. He slid his fingers through the soft curly hair. She was wet and ready for him. When he felt her legs wrap around his waist, pulling him closer, Cameron's control snapped.

He grasped her bottom with both hands, thrusting against her with urgent need. He tugged at the tiresome panties. "We need to get rid of these, sweetheart."

The low, savage words wrenched Jessie back to reality. *What was she doing?* She had only wanted one kiss, that's all she could allow herself. How quickly that kiss had spiraled into full-blown passion. Damn Tori and her punch!

Jessie caught Cameron's hand and her panties fell back in place. They were both breathing hard, staring at each other. His heavy-lidded eyes asked a question.

She didn't have the answer. She knew she couldn't blame the punch for her lapse. It was Cameron. It had always been Cameron. They'd felt the attraction when they were kids. But they weren't kids anymore and Cameron wasn't holding anything back. He wanted her.

And God help her, she wanted him. His kisses ignited a raging passion within her. She craved the feel of his hot mouth on her heated skin. She definitely had a weakness when it came to Cameron McCade.

But nothing had changed. He was leaving tomorrow. All he wanted was her body.

Jessie pushed away and jumped to her feet, keeping her eyes lowered. She tried desperately to restore order to her clothing and her emotions. Her fingers fumbled with the snaps. "I don't know what to say... I didn't mean to let it go that far."

Cameron grabbed her shoulders, hauling her against his chest, forcing her head back. His eyes blazed with frustration. "What's wrong, Jess? You want this as badly as I do. We're both adults, for Christ's sake."

Jerking out of his strong grasp, Jessie stood her ground. "You just don't get it, do you? There has to be more for me. I don't sleep around."

Cameron took a step closer. "I know you don't. There's something special between us; you know there is. We're good together."

"Yes, we're good together," she said, finally snapping the last snap on the side of the dress. She ran her fingers through her hair, trying to restore order to her appearance and to her thrumming body. "So good in fact, you make me forget everything."

"Is that bad?"

"Yes. No... I cannot, *will* not betray TR," she said quietly.

"How can you betray him? He's dead, Jess. Would he want you to stop living? Never enjoy a relationship with another man?"

Jessie shook her head. "No, he wouldn't mind if it were anyone but you."

Cameron's blue eyes widened in surprise. "What the hell is that supposed to mean?"

Smoothing the folds of her long skirt, she brushed cottonseed to the floor. Her emotions were jumbled and so was her brain. *She owed TR a lot. She'd married him without loving him, and she'd never given him children.*

Jessie couldn't tell Cameron the real reasons. She couldn't tell him she was afraid. Afraid she was falling in love with him again. Afraid she'd never stopped loving him. Afraid of the guilt and the regret.

Cameron grasped her shoulders again. She tried to wrench away, but he wouldn't let her. "What do you mean, Jess? Why would TR care that it's me?"

Jessie shook her head. "Because he hated your family. He never forgot about the feud."

"What feud? What in the world are you talking about?"

"The feud between your grandfather and TR's."

"Damn, Jess. That's ancient history. It has absolutely nothing to do with you and me."

Her heart ached so badly, she could scarcely breathe. "I'm sorry, Cameron. I just can't do this." She turned and ran out the door and into the night.

He watched her go. She was always running from him. Now he knew why. Had she loved TR so deeply? He ignored the stab of jealousy in his gut. How could he be jealous of a dead man?

Jessie might still love her husband, but she was liquid fire in his arms. Did she feel guilty about the sizzling attraction she felt for him? That must be it, he decided. Guilt was making Jessie run, from him and from life.

No woman had ever affected him like Jessie did. No woman had ever made him lose control like that. His body was strung as taut as a barbed wire fence. Clenching his fists, Cameron willed himself to relax.

If only he could stay longer. If only he didn't have to return to Houston so soon. Maybe he could help Jessie get past the guilt. She was too young to live the rest of her life alone. And there was something about her that touched him deeper than any woman ever had. The thought scared the living hell out of him, but it didn't scare him enough to make him leave her alone.

Mentally scanning his work schedule, he decided he would return to Salt Fork in a few weeks. One way or another, he and Jess would resolve this thing between them. One way or another.

CHAPTER SIX

On Monday morning, Jessie hurried to the shop and lost herself in work. She'd stayed home all day Sunday, trying not to think about Cameron, whether he had left yet, whether he would stop to say goodbye. She'd prayed he wouldn't. She didn't know how she could face him after what had happened at the party.

She didn't know how she could let him go, either. She was weak, damn it–weak where Cameron was concerned.

With an unspoken agreement, Sam took care of the customers, letting Jessie stay inside the office. She didn't know if he knew what was going on. She didn't explain and was grateful for his silence. Their relationship was simple, not complicated in the least. Why was it so complicated with Cameron?

After lunch, she and Sam were busy working on the carburetor of a customer's truck, when Jessie heard the unmistakable rumble of a diesel motor pull into the station. Her heart lurched for a second when she recognized Dallas McCade's pickup. Then she gave herself a mental shake. It wasn't Cameron; he was already back in Houston.

She glanced at Sam to see if he would take care of Dallas, or whoever had come from the Diamondback Ranch. She was in no mood to face anyone named McCade today. Sam's dark eyes gleamed as he started in the direction of the pumps. Jessie leaned around, curious to see who had sparked his interest, gasping when she realized it was Tori McCade.

Tori seemed a little young for Sam, a little too lively for such a serious man. Jessie turned back to work on the carburetor. Didn't she have enough to worry about? Tori was a big girl and could take care of herself.

After a few minutes, Jessie felt a tap on her shoulder. Tori stood at the front of the truck, peering with disgust at the greasy engine.

"How can you stand to work in all that muck?"

Jessie straightened and wiped her hands. "It's all I've ever known. Besides, I like engines."

Tori wrinkled her nose. "Why did you leave the party early without saying goodbye?"

"I had a headache, thanks to you and your punch."

"Was it the punch, or something else? Or *someone?* Maybe someone who's six-foot-three, has dark brown hair and blue eyes?"

Jessie stared at Tori. How much did she know? Was it only speculation? Or had Cameron told her something? "I don't know what you mean."

"Oh, *please*." Tori rolled her eyes. "Cameron spent a lot of time with you while he was home, or tried to. And I saw him practically drag you to the barn the other night. You were gone a good while. He came back alone and in a foul mood. I can put two and two together. You chickened out again, didn't you?"

Jessie leaned her elbows on the edge of the truck and hung her head. Maybe Cameron had the right idea about living in a large impersonal city. Tori wasn't going to shut up until she had her say. "So what if I did? I told you, it's complicated."

Tori squatted on her haunches and looked up at Jessie's face. "Only because you're making it that way."

"It doesn't matter," Jessie said. "He's gone and won't be back."

"I wouldn't be so sure of that," Tori said.

"Why not?"

"Yesterday, at breakfast, I mentioned the homecoming celebration next month. Cameron gave me this weird kind of look. He said he'd never been back for homecoming." Tori snorted. "Yeah, like that's a surprise."

"It doesn't mean anything. Him saying that." Jessie couldn't stop the leap in her pulse at the possibility of Cameron returning.

Tori smiled. "I think he'll come back in a couple of weeks, and I don't think it's because of homecoming."

Jessie's pulse slowed down; a heavy sensation gripped the back of her neck. If Cameron returned, it would just prolong the agony.

"What's wrong?" Tori asked. "Aren't you glad

Cameron's coming back? You still like him, don't you?"

Just then, Sam walked up, saving Jessie from having to reply.

"The truck's full," he told Tori. "I put it on the account."

Tori looked helplessly at Jessie. "I have to go."

Jessie watched her run to the truck, then eyed Sam with suspicion. "What have you done to that girl?"

Sam started adjusting the jets on the carburetor. "If you don't want me asking questions about your personal life, don't ask about mine."

"That certainly puts me in my place, doesn't it?"

Sam looked up, his dark eyes somber. "I know something's going on between you and McCade. A person would have to be blind not to see. Listen, Jessie. I admire how you've dealt with all the bumps thrown your way. McCade is just another bump. Don't worry so much. You'll deal with it, if you have to, just like you've dealt with all the rest. Hand me that screwdriver, will you?"

Jessie helped Sam finish the repair on the carburetor. His words rebounded in her mind, but he had it all wrong. Cameron wasn't a bump in her life; he was more like a mountain. And she didn't know how she was going to deal with him, or even if she'd get the chance.

By the middle of the next week, Jessie didn't have much time to think about Cameron and whether he would come back. Her financial situation had gone from bad to worse. She had fallen behind with the payments to the hospital and they were demanding settlement. Plus, her property taxes were due and she was already in arrears with them.

She had no other choice but to make that phone call to her lawyer and lease the mineral rights she held on the McCade property, so she could get her hands on some ready cash.

After talking to Mr. Bennett, Jessie called Ruth and asked to meet with her. An hour later, she and Cameron's mother were sitting in a booth at Sarah Sue's Café.

"Oh, Jessie, I wanted to thank you for the lovely yarns you gave me for my birthday. I'm going to crochet you an afghan with them."

"I'm glad you like them, but you don't have to make me an afghan. Although, I would love to have one, one of these days."

Ruth reached across the table and patted Jessie's hand. "I want to, dear. Your mother was one of my best friends. And you have a special place in my heart, you know that."

Jessie swallowed a lump in her throat. How would Ruth feel after her confession?

Ruth sat back and stirred her coffee. "Now, what was so all fired important that you had to see me ASAP?" She dropped the spoon and clapped her hands. "Is this about Cameron? Has he asked you to marry him?"

"*What*?" Jessie said, her stomach clenching at the thought. "Why would you think that?"

"He spent quite a bit of time with you while he was

at the ranch. And he said he's coming back for homecoming." Ruth shook her gray curls. "But of course, he wouldn't propose over the phone. Never mind, dear. Why did you want to see me?"

Jessie couldn't concentrate for a minute. Her thoughts were tumbling inside her head like juggler's balls gone all awry. What in the world had Cameron said to his mother and his sister? She couldn't deal with that at the moment; she had to tell Ruth what she'd done.

Taking a deep breath, Jessie took the plunge. "I have a confession to make."

Ruth frowned. "What kind of confession?"

"I'm so sorry, but I had to break the promise I made to you. And I'm afraid you're going to hate me when I tell you."

"I could never hate you, dear. Is this about the mineral rights?"

Jessie nodded. "I was forced to lease them to Copper River Oil. I didn't have a choice. I had to have the money, or I'd lose the garage."

"Well, you certainly couldn't do that, could you?"

Jessie sniffed back a tear. "No. It's my last link to my father."

Ruth shoved a napkin at Jessie. "Don't cry, dear. Just because you leased the land, doesn't mean they'll drill. At least, not right away."

"But with the oil situation like it is, they might," Jessie said. "You don't know how sorry I am. I hate breaking my promise."

"*I* understand, but Dallas will be furious. So will Austin. They both like to be in control of every facet concerning the ranching and agricultural aspects of the Diamondback." Ruth sipped her coffee. "Tyler and Cameron won't mind, too much. Neither will Tori. But Dallas..."

"Will you tell him for me?" Jessie blurted out. She usually wasn't a coward, but the thought of confessing to the big rancher made her more than a little queasy.

Ruth stared at her out of the same blue eyes she'd passed on to Cameron. Jessie couldn't tell what she was thinking, but she was obviously thinking hard about something.

Suddenly, Ruth smiled and nodded. "I'll tell him for you, dear. Don't you worry about a thing."

The night before the homecoming bonfire, Jessie found herself back at the garage after rushing home for a quick shower and bite to eat. The house had seemed too empty, her thoughts too restless and chaotic. Catching up on paperwork at the office had won out over spending another interminable evening at home.

Working the accounts was a breeze now that the money from the lease had been deposited into the bank. She was operating in the black once again, at least for a while. Ruth had taken the news remarkably well. Jessie wondered how Dallas had taken it.

After she'd settled her most pressing obligations, Jessie had begun thinking about Cameron again. She'd been on pins and needles these past couple of weeks, wondering if he would really come back. And what if he did? Everything was still the same between them. Even though she was afraid he'd stolen her heart again, she knew Cameron wanted nothing more than a roll in the hay. Or cottonseed, she thought with a blush.

All he wanted was a physical relationship. Sharing kisses with him and being left behind was bad enough. God help her, if she gave in to the raging passion between them. If Cameron returned, she hoped she would be strong enough to resist him.

The suspense was killing her. Jessie hadn't seen hide nor hair of a McCade since she'd spoken to Ruth. Surely, Cameron wouldn't come back so soon. He was a busy man. Why would he suddenly want to celebrate homecoming after all these years? She was flattering herself to think she was the lure to draw him home, no matter what Tori or Ruth said.

Just in case, Jessie thought maybe she should leave town, take some time off, avoid seeing him. But she couldn't do that. Not really. Besides, she enjoyed homecoming. Every year, she wrote a piece for the paper, outlining the events, including as many names of folks as she could cram into one article. People loved to see their names in print. It was a challenge to write the article year after year, to make it as interesting as possible. She couldn't let her feelings for Cameron interfere with that.

Tires crunching the pavement outside jolted Jessie from her thoughts. For a moment, she was afraid...

Afraid of what? Geez, Jess. You can't conjure Cameron out of thin air. She glanced out the window in the door and sighed in relief. Not a Jaguar, but the sheriff's black and white patrol car. Pasting a smile on her face, she went to greet him.

The sheriff touched his fingers to his Stetson. "Evening, Jessie."

"Hey, Roland. Something going on I should know about?"

She watched as he traced the toe of one shiny boot in the loose gravel on the pavement. Jessie's heart sank. She knew what was coming. Roland Burton had been asking her out for over a year. She liked him, but the chemistry wasn't right, at least not on her part.

The blustery November wind blew through her sweat suit. She shivered. "It's awfully cold out here. Why don't we go inside? We can talk over a hot cup of coffee."

"Sounds like a winner to me," he said, following her into the office.

Jessie handed Roland his cup and poured one for herself. She wrapped her cold fingers around the warm ceramic, hoping he'd get to the point soon. She knew it was difficult for him to gather the courage to ask her out and always felt like a heel when she refused his invitations.

The sheriff cleared his throat a couple of times, started to speak, then hurriedly sipped his coffee again. His cheeks were red, whether from embarrassment or the cold weather, Jessie couldn't tell.

Finally, he set his cup down and took a deep breath. "Tomorrow night's the big bonfire," he said in a rush. "I thought that maybe, that is–if you don't have other plans–maybe, you'd like to..."

Outside, a car pulled into the station, the tires squealing to a stop. Jessie's stomach plummeted to her feet. She knew who it was before the door opened. Her heart tumbled over when Cameron McCade filled the doorway, his eyes narrowed at the scene he'd interrupted.

An insane desire to hide behind Roland flashed through Jessie's mind. It was a sheriff's sworn duty to protect people, wasn't it? The look on Cameron's face was enough to scare anyone. On second thought, maybe she should try to protect Roland.

The sheriff stepped forward, hand outstretched. "Hello, Cameron. What brings you to town? Didn't think you'd be back so soon."

"I can see that." Cameron shook his hand, but his attention was focused on Jessie.

She hoped he wouldn't crush Roland's hand to a pulp. The menacing tone of his voice was unmistakable. She saw the confusion on Roland's face. The sheriff looked from Cameron to Jessie, then back again. It wasn't long before realization dawned. Snatching his Stetson from the desk, he said goodnight and fled.

The blood pounding in Cameron's head slowed down, and the red before his eyes faded away. He broke out in a cold sweat. *Jealousy and possessiveness*. They were new feelings, strange feelings. If he had any sense, he'd turn and run and never look back. Just like the sheriff.

The atmosphere sizzled in the small office. Jessie stood like a statue, her eyes opened wide. "Why did you come back?" Her raspy voice held a note of accusation.

Cameron also heard anguish in her words. Was he causing Jessie pain? When all he wanted was to hold her in his arms, take her to bed and make love to her until the passion between them was spent?

In two long strides, he was beside her. She backed against the file cabinet. He stepped closer.

"You know why I'm back. We need to finish what we started seventeen years ago." He touched a finger to her cheek, traced the smooth line of her jaw, eased his hand behind her neck and pulled her to him. Her trembling intensified and she put her hands on his chest as if to ward him off.

He caught her hands and moved them over his heart. "Feel my heartbeat, Jess. It's beating for you." He pressed his body against hers. "Feel how much I want you. I tried to stay away, but God help me, I couldn't."

His mouth claimed hers in fierce desire. Jessie moaned, holding back only for a second, knowing deep down that resistance was hopeless. She couldn't help it. She kissed him back, allowing the molten pleasure to seep through her veins. Her arms crept around his neck. For one long moment, she gave in to the encircling warmth and strength of his embrace.

Cameron's hands became more insistent. He was going mad with the need to feel her bare body against his, her silky skin touching him, shoulder to shoulder, thigh to thigh. He grasped Jessie's bottom and lifted her against him, thrusting his arousal between her thighs. He felt her heat and wanted inside her.

Suddenly, she stiffened. Cameron knew she was remembering. Remembering the reasons why she couldn't do this or *thought* she couldn't. Inwardly groaning, he leaned his forehead against hers. She tried to wriggle away, but he tightened his arms around her. "Don't run from me, Jess."

"I can't do this... I promised..." Jessie squeezed her eyes shut. A tear trickled down her cheek.

Cameron kissed it away. He pulled her face into his shoulder and kissed the top of her head. "You're right, sweetheart. We can't do this. Not yet." He handed her a large white handkerchief. "Dry your tears. We need to talk."

Jessie dabbed at her eyes. Cameron's spicy scent clung to the handkerchief, assailing her senses, enticing her back into his arms. She had dreaded his return, but now that he was here, her feelings and emotions were jumbled. Again. She folded the snowy white linen and gave it back. "Okay... I'm okay. Let's talk."

Capturing her wrists, Cameron kissed the delicate undersides. He sat on the edge of the desk and drew her between his legs. Jessie felt her cheeks burn and swallowed hard. "I think I'll sit down," she said, diving for the swivel chair.

Cameron squatted beside her and placed his hand on her knee. Jessie gripped the arms of the chair.

"There's something between us, Jess. You feel it; I feel it. You want to ignore it, but I can't. Not anymore. I don't think either of us can ignore it."

"There's nothing between us. There can never be anything between us," Jessie declared vehemently. "Oh God, why did you have to come back? I don't need this."

"Maybe you do need this. I know *I* do. I went back

to Houston and tried to push you out of my mind. I can't sleep, Jess. I'm a bear at work. I can't concentrate. All I can think about is you. Hell, it's as bad or worse than when we were kids. That night, after the prom, as soon as I kissed you, I wanted more."

Jessie hung her head. "You must not have wanted me very much. You left town without saying goodbye."

"I said goodbye up on Lover's Point."

And took my heart with you. Why was he telling her this? It only made it worse. It didn't matter that she loved Cameron, had always loved him. He didn't love her. He only wanted her in bed.

Jessie sighed. "We said our goodbyes on Lover's Point and you never looked back. No calls, no letters. A few times you stopped for gas, but even then... seventeen years is a long time, Cameron. I tried to forget this *thing* between us. You made it perfectly clear that I had no place in your life or your plans. I married TR and tried to be a good wife." *Tried, but failed*, she thought miserably. "Why did you come back? Yes, there's an extraordinary chemistry between us, but what then? I would have thought there were plenty of women in Houston you could... you know."

Cameron swore silently. She wasn't making this easy for him. Hell, he wasn't sure why he'd come back.

Seeing her sitting there, chin held high, and knowing that below the surface a fire burned for him, ready to ignite if only she would let him fan it, Cameron was suddenly unsure of everything. Would one night, one week in bed with Jessie be enough? He had a sinking suspicion that he was in over his head and powerless to stop it.

Easing out of the crouch, Cameron leaned both hands on the arms of the chair, effectively trapping Jessie. God, she smelled good. He took her chin in his palm and brushed her lips with his thumb, tightening his grip when she tried to pull away. "We're good together, Jess. You said I make you forget. Let me help you forget. You can't keep living in the past."

"I'm not living in the past."

"Aren't you?" He pulled her to stand in front of him. "I want you so much." He kissed the sensitive spot just below her ear. "I turned my back on you when we were kids. I don't think I can turn back now."

Jessie tilted her head. Cameron's warm lips nibbled her earlobe, then nuzzled the length of her neck to her collarbone. He dipped his tongue into the silky hollow, then started back up again.

Why couldn't she just relax and enjoy this? Cameron's words reverberated in her mind. Was she living in the past? TR was dead. Nothing could bring him back. Nothing could change what she'd done. She'd married TR, but hadn't loved him. Cameron was her first love, her only love. *Her true love*. But oh, the guilt weighed her down.

She pushed at his massive chest as hard as she could. "We have to stop. I can't do this. Shouldn't..."

"Damn it, Jess." Cameron grasped her shoulders, barely restraining himself from shaking her. "TR is gone. Let him go."

"I know TR is dead, but a wife should be loyal to her husband... to his memory. His battles were my battles...

are my battles."

"Even when you don't know what you're fighting for? You said yourself you don't know what the feud was about. It's not your feud. Hell, it wasn't even TR's. It was about something that happened years ago when our grandfathers were young."

"Do you know why they were fighting?" For some reason, the answer was important. Jessie felt like she was in a dark tunnel and had just spotted a pinpoint of light. If she found out the reason for the feud, then she'd have one less thing to feel guilty about. Maybe she could move on and not feel as if she were betraying her husband.

"I don't know the reason, but we can find out." Cameron grabbed her hand and started for the door.

"Where are we going?"

"To the ranch. My mother will know what that damned feud was about."

Ruth sat at the old oak table in her kitchen. She looked from Cameron to Jessie, then back to Cameron again. "I haven't thought about the feud in a long time. Grandma told me about it when I first married your father, but nobody mentioned it much after that."

Jessie sat across from Ruth, waiting impatiently. What could have happened to make TR's grandfather hate the McCades so much that his grandson carried on the feud after his death? Suddenly, she wasn't sure she wanted to know. Ignorance was sometimes bliss. She didn't want to betray TR, but it was time to move forward. She'd been given another chance with Cameron. She couldn't let it slip through her fingers. But the guilt... she had to get past the guilt.

Ruth folded a dishcloth, smoothing the material with her palms. "Grandma said it was the silliest thing, really. She couldn't understand why the men acted so stupid." She reached over and patted Cameron's hand. "Nothing personal, dear. Men just can't help themselves. Not that you act stupid, at least, not often."

Jessie shot a look at Cameron to see his reaction. His eyes held a glint of amusement. All the McCades adored their mother. That had to be a point in their favor.

"Anyway," Ruth continued, "Grandma said it was just a misunderstanding. 'All's fair in love and war,' if you get my drift?"

Cameron took a deep breath. Probably praying for patience, Jessie thought.

"No, we don't get your meaning," he said. "Tell us what happened."

"Well, Grandma was engaged to Travis Devine before she married Grandpa."

"TR's grandfather?" Jessie asked.

Ruth nodded, her cheeks turning pink as if she were embarrassed.

"So what?" Cameron said. "They obviously broke up and she married Grandpa."

Ruth shook her head. "There was a little more to it than that. The night before the wedding, Grandpa persuaded her to run off with him. It caused quite a scandal. Travis was left standing at the altar, so to speak.

He never forgave Grandpa or Grandma."

"Why didn't she just end the engagement?" Jessie asked.

"She couldn't. Everything was in place. It had something to do with the land. *This* land. Grandma was an only child. She brought a good portion of the Diamondback Ranch, only it wasn't called that back then, to her marriage. Grandpa came home from the war and swept her off her feet. They fell in love, but Travis wouldn't release her from the betrothal. He wanted the land, you see."

"Are you sure he didn't love her?" Jessie said.

"Travis Devine never loved anyone but himself," Ruth said. "He married TR's grandmother shortly after the scandal. *Her* parents had money. Not a whole lot, but enough."

"So why did Grandpa sell old man Devine the mineral rights?" Cameron asked.

"He was trying to smooth things over with Travis. Grandpa had a chance to expand the ranch, but was short on cash." Ruth shot Jessie a mischievous and conspiring look, no doubt thinking about Jessie's recent lack of cash flow. "Travis had become something of a recluse, always making threats against the McCades, obsessed with the Diamondback Ranch. Grandpa offered the mineral rights on the northeast portion of the ranch, the part that adjoins the Devine place. It was sort of like an olive branch."

"It didn't help though, did it?" Jessie said.

"No, it didn't. Travis bought the rights and held them over Grandpa's head, always threatening to lease them to one of the big oil companies. He knew Grandpa would be powerless to stop them from drilling on the land."

"So why didn't he make good on his threats?" Cameron said.

"Luckily, the big companies were too busy drilling off-shore. They haven't bothered looking for oil around here in years. Only until recently..." Ruth trailed off as she looked again at Jessie.

Cameron scooted back his chair. "I know about Jessie and the mineral rights."

"You do?" Ruth asked.

He nodded. "We talked about it when I was here last time, remember? Anyway, thanks for telling us about the feud. I'm going to take Jessie home now."

"My truck's at the garage," Jessie said.

"Then I'll take you there."

He guided her out the door, his hand resting on the small of her back. His touch sent shivers down to her toes. She tried not to blush at Ruth's knowing smile.

On the road to town, Jessie sat in silence. The feud had happened so long ago; it seemed foolish now. True love had won out over greed. TR's grandfather had nursed the grudge because he'd lost the land. He had taught TR to hate and mistrust the McCades. Sighing, Jessie knew she had never hated the McCades. In fact, she'd lost her heart to one when she'd been very young.

She turned her head slightly and studied Cameron's profile. The lights from the instrument panel cast a soft glow over his rugged features. He caught her eye and winked, setting butterflies loose in her stomach. He was dangerously handsome, the attraction between them almost frightening.

Cameron was right. She *had* been living in the past. With Ruth's explanation, Jessie finally understood TR's hatred toward the McCades.

"Why so quiet?" Cameron asked, glancing at her.

Because I want you so much it scares me. Of course, she couldn't tell him that. "I was thinking how much time and energy TR wasted on that feud. Travis Devine's hatred affected TR's life and mine."

"Does this mean you're going to put the feud to rest?" he asked.

Jessie swallowed hard and nodded. "Yes, I guess I am."

"Good. I'm glad, Jess." Cameron's smile burned a hole right through her midsection.

"Does this mean you'll sell Dallas the mineral rights?"

The muscles in the back of her neck tightened. Letting go of the feud was one thing; letting go of those mineral rights was something else. "No, I've told you before. I'll never sell the mineral rights."

"Why not? You realize the feud was pointless. Why not let Dallas buy back the rights?"

"I promised TR, and that's one promise I won't break. I hate breaking promises. I hated breaking the one I made to your mother. I had to lease the rights, you know. I had to make that phone call."

"You did? She seems to be taking it well," Cameron said.

"I still hate that I had to do it."

"Try not to worry about it, Jess. You did what you had to do."

The lights of Salt Fork were straight ahead. Cameron turned into the station and parked next to Jessie's pickup. He got out, walked around to open Jessie's door and helped her out.

"So what happens now, Jess?" he asked.

"I'm not sure. You're the one who always has a plan."

He frowned. "Right, a plan. Would you believe I don't have one this time?"

That made her smile. "Wow, this must be a first for you."

Cameron stepped close and touched her cheek in a gentle caress. "Help me, Jess. I don't know where to go from here. I want you so much, I hurt. But I can't see my way through. For once in my life, I'm acting on impulse. I don't know what I really want. Not only in my personal life, but my professional life as well."

"Cameron, I–"

He placed a finger over her lips. "Help me find the way, Jess. Nothing feels right anymore. All I know is that when I'm with you, everything feels better."

Cameron gathered her in his arms and kissed her tenderly. "Help me, sweetheart."

Jessie knew she was fighting a losing battle. She didn't want to betray TR, but Cameron was right. It was time to move forward. She'd been given a second chance. And Cameron seemed open to explore what they felt for each other. She couldn't let it slip through her fingers.

Jessie wiggled free from Cameron's hold. He said he wanted to continue where they'd left off. Then maybe they needed to go back to where it had all begun.

"Jess?" Confusion and desire burned in his blue eyes. "Let me love you, please."

If only he could. Jessie took his big hand in hers and tugged. "Come on, Cameron."

He hung back. "Where are we going?"

"Lover's Point."

"Lover's Point? Why?"

She placed his hand on her heart. "Because that's where all of this started."

"And that's where you think it should end?"

"Not end," Jessie said. "Begin. Let's make a new beginning."

"I'd like that, Jess. I'd like that a lot."

CHAPTER SEVEN

*T*he drive to Lover's Point took less than ten minutes. Ten long minutes that had Jessie wrestling with second, third and fourth thoughts. Could she put years of self-blame and sorrow behind her and move on? Or would this just cause more inner turmoil?

Cameron turned off the main road and drove up the bluff leading to Lover's Point. He parked the Jag on the ridge overlooking the deep canyon and cut the motor and the lights. The moon glowed brightly in the dark sky and a trail of wispy clouds floated across its silver face.

Jessie gripped the door handle, ready to hurl herself from the car. She wasn't ready... she wasn't sure...

"It's all right, Jess. We're not going to do anything until both of us want to."

Jessie's heart turned over at the tenderness in his voice. She licked her dry lips. "It's silly, but I'm nervous."

"I'm a little nervous, too." Cameron leaned against the doorframe and faced her in the darkness. "The last time I was up here, it was with you. You were nervous then, too. You'd never been to Lover's Point. You'd never been kissed."

"You remember it was my first kiss?" *How sweet was that?* Maybe he cared for her more than he realized.

"I remember feeling glad I was your first. You were so innocent and so damned young." Cameron snagged her gaze, his eyes tender and hot at the same time. "I remember a lot of things about that night."

"Like what?" Jessie tucked one leg beneath her, positioning herself toward him.

"Like I was glad I asked you to the prom. I was glad you accepted my invitation."

"But I was your last resort," Jessie said. "The prom was only a few days away. You'd broken up with Patti and there was no one left to ask."

His eyes burned into hers. "You weren't my last resort, Jess." His deep voice wrapped around her like a caress.

"I wasn't?" Her heart thudded in her ears.

"Not by a long shot," he said. "There were several girls in Girard and Cactus Gap who would've gone with me. You were *not* my last resort."

"Really?" Jessie's stomach did a belly flop. All these years she'd believed she was his last choice. That it had been a total fluke when he'd asked her to the prom. She'd been wrong. What else had she been wrong about?

"Yes, really." Cameron leaned closer. "Know what

else I remember about that night?"

Jessie leaned closer, too; she couldn't help herself. "What do you remember?" she asked softly.

"I remember how beautiful you were in that dress. You looked so grown up. And *sexy*. I'd never seen you out of your coveralls."

Cameron reached for her and slipped his fingers behind her neck, drawing her across the console until they were only millimeters apart. "I'd give anything to see you out of your coveralls again." She felt his warm breath on her lips.

"*Why* did you come back?" Jessie asked, searching his eyes in the darkness.

"I couldn't stay away, Jess. I just couldn't stay away." He ground out the words as he clamped his mouth on hers.

Jessie's heart shifted in her chest. She gave in to the whirlpool of passion, kissing Cameron like she'd been longing to do, tasting him, savoring the feel of him.

After a couple of minutes, Cameron pulled back and smiled a smile so sexy, so intimate, whatever barriers Jessie had erected crashed and burned.

"This is good, Jess. This feels right." He pushed the bucket seat away from the steering wheel and hauled Jessie onto his lap. He wrapped his arms tightly around her and brushed his lips across hers, back and forth, teasing, taunting.

Jessie's breasts grew heavy. Her nipples ached to be touched. She felt Cameron's arousal thrusting against her. She wriggled until they fit snugly together. The layers of clothing only intensified the wanting, the longing, the desire.

Cameron scattered fleeting kisses over her eyelids, her cheeks, the tip of her nose. He kissed the corners of her mouth, nipped her chin, caressed her face with his lips, but never tasted her fully.

Jessie thought she might die if he didn't kiss her, *really* kiss her. His words echoed in her ears. This *did* feel good; it felt so right to be in his arms again. She tried to catch his mouth, but he held her captive with one strong hand tangled in her hair.

"Please, Cameron." A liquid heat gathered low in her stomach.

"Tell me what you want," he said, quickly dipping his tongue into her mouth, only to retreat again.

"Kiss me. Please kiss me," she said.

With his hands on either side of her face, he slanted his head and fastened his mouth on hers, plunging deeply, grinding his lips against her softness. He shifted his lower body to stroke her from below. She groaned into his mouth.

Cameron cupped one breast, kneading gently through the layers of cloth. "I want you, Jess. Let me make love to you."

Jessie knew if she rejected Cameron now, she would regret it for the rest of her life. She was so tired of the turmoil and self-reproach. She was ready for a new beginning with Cameron. She loved him. She'd loved him forever. Maybe she could make him love her back.

Cameron touched her cheek. "Jess?"

She caught his hand and kissed his palm. His blue eyes glittered in the dark interior of the car.

"Is that a yes?" he asked.

"Yes, oh, yes!" She couldn't resist him any longer; she captured his mouth in another heart-stopping kiss. "Let's go to my house."

He smiled his killer smile. "Excellent idea." Kissing her one more time, Cameron set her from him and started the car.

"It's getting late," Jessie said, buckling her seat belt. "I'll need my pickup in the morning for work."

"All right. We'll go back and get your truck. Then I'll follow you home." He leaned over and took her mouth again before reluctantly breaking contact.

They didn't talk on the way to the garage. Cameron stopped the car beside her pickup. "Go on, Jess. The quicker we get to your house, the quicker we can get naked and into bed."

The provocative words flowed over her like warm honey. Her body pulsed with desire. She didn't know how she made it to her truck; she was sure her feet never touched the ground.

Jessie kept glancing in her rear view mirror on the drive home, mesmerized by Cameron's headlights. Feelings of elation alternated with misgivings. This was a big step. Could she handle the aftermath? Could she make Cameron love her?

She parked at the back of the house and so did Cameron. He stood close behind as she opened the door, then followed her into the dark kitchen. Jessie switched on the lights and made a beeline for the heater. She struck a match and the blue flame leapt to life.

"Sorry it's so cold," she said. "I turn everything off before I go to work. I better light the other heaters, so we won't freeze to death."

Cameron reached for her. "I don't think we need to worry about that."

Suddenly shy, Jessie slipped from his arms and dashed to the living room. "You don't realize how cold it actually is. I won't be long," she called.

After a few minutes, she came back to the kitchen and stopped in the doorway. Cameron stood by the stove, warming his hands, his presence filling the room. He turned to warm his backside, and his eyes fastened on hers.

"Come on over here, Jess." He held out his arms, and she walked straight into his embrace.

Cameron enveloped her in a bear hug, slowly rotating so she could be warmed by the fire. She wrapped her arms around his waist and rested her head against his chest. For a moment, they stood just like that, taking advantage of the heat from the stove. Soon, a different kind of heat built between them.

Jessie looked up. Cameron's eyes were heavy with desire. Her stomach jittered nervously. "Do you want a drink?"

He shook his head and gave her a smile so sensual, it stole the breath from her lungs. "No, all I want is you." He slid his hands to her bottom and pulled her hard against his body.

"There's something I need to tell you," Jessie said.

He rubbed his hands up and down her spine. "What is it, sweetheart?"

"I haven't... done this in a long time."

Cameron's hands stopped rubbing. "Exactly how long do you mean?"

"I haven't been with anyone since TR." She thought she might as well confess it all. "I haven't been with anyone except TR."

Cameron moved his hands again. "It'll be good between us. I'll make it good. I promise." He kissed her, dipping into her sweetness. His tongue swirled around her liquid warmth.

Jessie closed her eyes, tilting her head back. Her lower body readied itself, growing damp, throbbing to be filled. Her knees sagged. She kept from falling by clasping her arms more tightly around Cameron's waist. How many years had she dreamed of this moment?

Cameron hooked an arm under her legs, lifting Jessie with ease. She grabbed hold around his neck and nestled her head in the crook of his shoulder.

"Where's your bed?" he asked, his voice ragged.

"Through there." She motioned toward the living room. "But it's going to be freezing," she warned.

"Not for long."

With quick, determined strides, he found the bedroom. He set Jessie on the big double bed and flicked on the lamp, then shrugged out of his jacket. The coldness hit him like a blast from the Arctic.

"Damn, you're right," he said, blowing on his hands. He sat next to Jessie and briskly rubbed her arms. "These sheets are like ice."

Jessie made a quick decision. She handed two pillows to Cameron and grabbed the quilt. "Follow me." Now that she'd made up her mind, her shyness evaporated. Despite the frigid temperature, her body was on fire.

In the living room, she spread the quilt in front of the heater. She took the pillows from Cameron, dropped them on the pallet and pulled an afghan from the sofa. Closing the distance between them, she wound her arms around his neck and kissed his chin. "Is this better?"

"Yes, ma'am." Cameron kissed her deeply, his tongue exploring and tangling with hers. After a few delicious minutes, he knelt and grasped her round bottom, kneading the firm flesh through the sweatpants, placing kisses across her fleece-covered abdomen, pushing the pants down her legs and following their path with little nips and kisses.

Jessie kicked off her shoes and stepped from the puddled heap of fabric. She ran her fingers through Cameron's crisp brown hair and gasped when she felt the heat from his mouth between her thighs. Even through her panties, the sensation caused an unbearable tension to coil in the pit of her stomach. She pushed forward, seeking closer contact.

"Cameron..."

"Easy, Jess. We have the whole night before us." He pushed the edge of her sweatshirt slowly upward, trailing his tongue and lips over the bared skin. He lingered over her breasts and suckled the nipples through the lacy bra. Cameron eased the shirt over her head and returned his attention to the lace-captive flesh. With one arm supporting the small of her back, he unfastened the bra, releasing her breasts, feasting his eyes on the enticing curves and rosy brown nipples.

"Beautiful. You're so damned beautiful." He bent to kiss each nipple, flicking his tongue, nipping with his lips, blowing his hot breath across them until they beaded. Jessie arched her back, offering herself, moaning deeply in her throat.

Cameron felt himself throbbing with need, and the pressure against his zipper begged for release. He'd never failed to pleasure a woman, but Jessie was different. Special. She had always been different. Always been special. Knowing how long it had been for her, what value she placed on sharing her body–all of it was driving him over the edge too damn fast. The fierce need to possess her scared the hell out of him. He had never felt this way about a woman. Never.

"Please, Cameron," Jessie pleaded, reaching for him.

Still on his knees, he buried his face between the soft swell of her breasts. He trailed his tongue along the curves, teasing the nipples, bathing the tips with the flat of his tongue. Jessie's body jerked with reaction.

Cameron gently lowered her to the pallet, never breaking contact. Jessie frantically pulled his shirt from his jeans. She plunged her hands under the fabric, pressing her palms and fingers over his warm skin. It wasn't enough. She groaned in frustration and tugged the shirt upwards.

Cameron's control slipped a notch. Her small hands on his body made him want to immediately thrust inside her. "Slow down, sweetheart. We need to slow down."

"I don't want to slow down. I need you. Help me get your shirt off."

Cameron sat up and pulled the offending garment over his head. Jessie's impatience was contagious. He hooked his fingers under the elastic of her panties and peeled them down the length of her long, shapely legs. With his eyes on hers, he reached for his zipper and unfastened his jeans. Pushing them down, he shucked them out of the way.

Stretching out beside her, his heated gaze traveled the length of her body. He hadn't thought it possible, but he hardened even more.

Jessie laid her palms flat against his chest. Her emerald eyes shimmered with passion. She wet her lips with the tip of her tongue. "Now, Cameron. Take me now. Please."

Her whispered plea shattered what was left of his control. It was impossible to wait another moment. Later they could leisurely taste and touch, savor each other's bodies. Right now, he had to have her and make her his. He wanted to feel her inner muscles contract as she accepted him into her body. He grabbed his jeans and pulled a small plastic package from the pocket.

Jessie stared at the packet. Protection wasn't necessary. But now wasn't the time to tell Cameron she couldn't have children. She didn't want anything to spoil their lovemaking.

Taking the square packet from him, she brushed her arm against his hot erection. Deliberately, she brushed him again as she got to her knees. "We really don't need this."

Cameron's eyes dilated and his nostrils flared. "You're protected?"

Jessie tossed the condom aside. "Absolutely." It wasn't really a lie.

For a moment, she knelt there and just looked at him. He was big and hard and beautiful. She bent and swirled her tongue over and around the rigid tip of his erection. Her stomach contracted in feminine triumph when Cameron clutched her head, threading his fingers in her hair, groaning his desire. She moistened the length of him with her lips, caressing him with her tongue, teasing a bit before finally taking him in her mouth.

"You're killing me, Jess."

She lifted her head and smiled. "Am I?" Slowly, sensuously, she slid her hand up and down his length, then cupped the velvety sacs in her palms.

Cameron growled as he pushed her back onto the pallet. He followed her down and covered her with his body. He closed his eyes, striving for control, luxuriating in the feel of her naked against him. He gripped the sides of her head and plunged his tongue into her willing mouth, ravishing the warm interior, capturing her lips with his teeth, biting gently, sucking hard.

With his knee, he wedged open her thighs and entered her, pushing until he was secured. He waited a minute, holding his breath, afraid he'd explode. He wanted to make it good for Jessie, because it was damn sure good for him. Slowly, he began to move.

Jessie clasped her legs around Cameron's waist and held on tightly. She'd been living for this moment all of her life. She kissed the corded muscles of his neck. His lips compressed in a tight line. He slid his arms behind to grasp her buttocks, hammering into her again and again. She welcomed his weight and met each powerful plunge with an upward thrust. She relished the feel of her breasts crushed beneath his chest, the driving force as their bodies joined.

They quickly discovered their own unique rhythm. Coming together, pulling apart. Breaths scorching, sweat glistening. Muscles tensing, flexing. Jessie soared on the precipice of release, the magic in sight, the urgency mounting, the tension agonizing.

Cameron raised up and pushed deeper, slowly pulling out to prolong the sweet torture, then thrusting again until he was buried to the hilt.

When Jessie finally cried out, her body overtaken by a powerful orgasm, Cameron dropped his head to the pillow, whispering encouragement, finding his own release as she strained against him. Together they hurtled through time that had stopped. Swirling in the violence of their passion, free-falling back to earth, they lay in the aftermath of their desire, waiting for the pounding of their hearts to slow and their throbbing bodies to still.

The next day, bright autumn sunlight cast dusty beams through the high windows of Kincaid's Garage. Jessie was busy working on Cy Jackson's tractor. She had flushed the radiator and was now checking the thermostat. She tried not to think about the night before, but couldn't help herself. Happiness and despondency warred inside her.

No way did she regret the lovemaking. It had been wonderful. Everything she had imagined plus some. She blushed when she remembered Cameron's insatiable desire. *And her own.* As if they were trying to make up for all the years they had been apart. Finally, exhausted and replete, they had fallen asleep in each other's arms.

Jessie had awakened on the cold hard pallet in the early morning hours, turning to seek the warmth of Cameron's body, only to find emptiness. He had left without saying goodbye. She dragged her love-sore body to bed and crawled between icy sheets, flipping on the electric blanket. It wasn't long until her feet were toasty, but nothing could warm the chill clutching her heart.

What had she expected? She had known Cameron wouldn't stay; leaving was what he was good at. No, Jessie wasn't sorry she'd made love with Cameron. It had been beautiful and right. She loved him more than ever, but what would happen now? What did he want from her? What more was she willing to give?

Jessie reached for a wrench, when suddenly, large hands spun her around until she was lodged between the tractor and a hard muscled male body. Before she could utter a greeting or protest, Cameron's mouth crushed down on hers, taking her with a savage passion, his tongue tangling with her tongue, renewing the erotic rhythm they'd discovered last night.

Jessie's doubts and fears faded to the background. Her heart sang joyously. *Cameron was back.* She plastered her body to his rugged frame.

Cameron drew her closer, gripping her bottom, lifting her a little, so he could rub against her. He felt her tremble in his arms, sigh into his mouth. She was so responsive. So giving. So sexy.

He set Jessie on her feet and kept his arms around her. "Good morning, sweetheart." He kissed her nose and forehead. God, he'd hated leaving her on their makeshift pallet. The temptation to stay and wake her with his kisses, bring her to pleasure as the sun peeked in the east, plunge himself into her inviting heat–it had been almost more than he could resist.

But he hadn't dared spend the entire night with her. If they had been in Houston, it would have been different. They could have stayed in bed morning, noon, and night. As it was, he knew his mother would have enough to talk about knowing he'd taken Jessie home and stayed so late. So he'd forced himself to leave, ignoring the compelling urge to take her again, brand her as his. Feelings of protectiveness battled with feelings of possessiveness. He'd been shocked by the primitive need to claim this woman as his own.

Jessie slipped out of Cameron's embrace and stood, hands on hips, glaring at him. "Why did you leave me without saying goodbye?"

"Because you were sleeping so soundly, I hated to disturb you." He reached for her, wanting to gather her in his arms again.

She pushed away, putting the tool bench between them.

"Aw, Jess. What are you doing? There's no need to play games. We're past that, I hope. Give me another kiss."

Playing games? She didn't think so. Too much was at stake, namely her heart. But she couldn't tell Cameron that. They were beginning anew. Starting over. She had to tread carefully. Maybe he was right. Maybe she *was* playing a game.

She chose her words with care. "Last night was special for me. When I woke up and you weren't there... I felt... bad."

Cameron stepped around the bench, taking her in his arms. "I'm sorry, Jess. I only want to make you feel good. We *are* good together, aren't we?"

"Yes," she said, keeping her eyes on his chest. *But for how long?* The silent question made her want to cry.

Cameron grasped the nape of her neck and gently tugged her hair, tilting her head back until she met his gaze. "Next time, I'll be sure to say goodbye before I leave your bed." He skimmed his tongue gently across her lips, lightly tasting before devouring her with his mouth.

Jessie closed her eyes and put her arms around Cameron's waist. It was a heady sensation to feel him tremble with need for her, just as she trembled for him. They *were* good together. Surely, that had to count for something. And what had he meant by 'next time'? Was he staying around for a while?

Jessie broke the embrace when she heard a door slam. She didn't want Sam to catch her in Cameron's arms. "I have to get back to work."

Reluctantly, Cameron let her go. He nodded to Garza as the man walked up.

"Morning," Sam said, eyeing them strangely. "Finished with the tractor, Jessie?"

"It still needs antifreeze," she said.

"I'll take care of it."

Cameron grabbed Jessie's arm and hauled her outside. He hated her working so closely with Garza. What the hell was the matter with him? He was jealous, that's what. And possessive. First, the sheriff. Now, Garza. Who next?

After tasting the delights of Jessie's body last night, he wanted more. *Now.* But that was impossible, so he crammed his hands in his pockets instead of dragging her slender body close.

Jessie watched the desire burn in Cameron's eyes. The knuckles of his clenched fists turned white before he buried them in his jeans. For a moment, she was afraid he was going to kiss her out here in front of God and everybody. That would certainly give the town something to talk about, especially after he left. She readjusted her hat, stuffing her hair under the brim. The draft from the cold morning breeze hit her face. The promise of winter floated in the chilled air. She shifted her weight from one foot to the other, waiting for Cameron to speak. It was getting cold, the silence awkward. Did last night mean anything to him? They'd finished what they'd started on Lover's Point. How long before he returned to Houston? She had to prepare herself. He would leave. It was inevitable.

"Did you want to tell me something in particular? Or did you drag me out here to freeze my bottom off?" she said. To hell with melancholy thoughts. She needed to enjoy this time with Cameron. It was all she would have.

"I want to go to the bonfire tonight and I want you to go with me."

Jessie's jaw dropped. *Cameron wanted to take her to the bonfire?* She really shouldn't place too much importance on it, or let herself hope, but she couldn't help the happy little bubble dancing inside. She smiled and kissed his cheek. "I'd love to go. Say about six-thirty?"

"That's fine. And this time, I'll pick you up. No arguments." He grasped her wrist, pulled her to him and kissed her hard. Jessie's eyes widened in surprise. She halfheartedly attempted to push away, even while her mouth melted beneath his onslaught.

Finally, he let her go. "I'll be by your house at six-thirty. Be ready for me."

Cameron left her standing by the garage doors, gasping for breath, her eyes dreamy with passion. If she looked at him like that tonight when he picked her up, they would be late for the bonfire.

CHAPTER EIGHT

*J*essie was waiting on her porch, ready to leave when Cameron pulled up. She hurried to the car and hopped in. Her smile was strained when she greeted him. No time for kisses, no time for passion. They wouldn't be late to the bonfire, damn it. He wondered what was wrong.

As he turned onto the highway, she started digging in her purse.

"Did you forget something?" he asked. "Need to go back to the house?"

"Nope, I found it." She pulled out a small spiral pad attached to a long ribbon and tied it around her neck like a necklace. Then she fastened a ballpoint to the ribbon and snapped her purse shut.

"What's with the pad and pen? Are you going to take notes or something?"

"Yes. For the paper."

"For the paper?"

"The newspaper. Every year, I do a story on the homecoming festivities."

"You do keep busy, don't you?"

Again, that strained smile. "I like to be busy."

Cameron drummed his fingers on the steering wheel, racking his brain for something to say. They were acting like strangers, which was ridiculous. Last night, they had been naked in bed. Engaged in the best sex he'd ever had. He'd thought it had been good for Jessie, too.

He glanced at her. She was staring out the window. It had been a big step for her to go to bed with him. Maybe she regretted it, or maybe she just felt uncomfortable and awkward. He didn't know what to say.

They continued the ride in silence. On the edge of town, Cameron slowed down. As always, the bonfire ceremony took place in the big field across from the high school. Now, there was Jessie's clinic sharing the space. He wanted another look at the medical clinic. He'd been thinking about it ever since Jessie had given him the grand tour.

He parked near the other cars and trucks.

"Something wrong?" he asked, then couldn't help himself. "Are you sorry about last night?"

"No." She turned and faced him. "No, I'm not sorry about last night."

"So what's bothering you?"

Jessie sighed deeply. "Nothing. I'm just being silly. Come on, let's go." She was out the door before he could ask more questions.

"Wait, Jess," he called, jogging after her.

Jessie stopped and stared straight ahead.

"You going to tell me what's going on?"

"Nothing's going on. I'm fine, I promise."

Cameron resisted the urge to drag her in his arms and kiss away her worries. He needed to be cautious; he was swimming in dangerous waters here. He had no plan. He was going on gut instinct and didn't know where it would lead him.

"Ready for some small town fellowship?" Jessie asked with a more natural smile playing on her lips.

It was Cameron's turn to sigh. "Some things never change, do they?"

"No, they don't."

There was a sad tone to her voice, he didn't understand. She took his hand and they walked toward the crowd gathered near the center of the field.

The mayor had the honor of lighting the bonfire. The cheerleaders started a round of yells as soon as the huge pile of lumber, mesquite and large tumbleweeds ignited.

Cameron watched the twenty-foot blaze flicker in the darkness. The orange and blue flames roared upward and reached for the night sky. He and Jessie stood a short distance away, watching the sparks burst, listening to the sizzling sounds, welcoming the heat from the small inferno. The weather had turned blustery cold.

With his hand on the back of her neck, he guided her through the throng of people, stopping to exchange greetings with old friends and teachers. Nothing had changed, just as he'd said. Homecoming was still the highlight of the football season with the bonfire, the game, the king and queen, and the dance.

"Hey, Cameron. You old son-of-a-gun!" Lester Smith slapped him on the shoulder.

Cameron shook the hand thrust toward him. Lester had been his best buddy in high school. He'd moved to St. Louis after college. "How've you been?"

"Fine, just fine," Lester said, pumping his arm up and down like an old-fashioned water pump. His eyes widened. "And Jessie! Haven't seen you in ages."

"Hey, Lester," she said in greeting.

"Don't tell me you two are a couple?" Lester finally let go of Cameron's hand. "Seems like the last time I saw y'all was... at the prom... Hey, you're not *married*, are you?"

Cameron's hand dropped away from Jessie. "No, we're not married."

As she listened to Cameron talk to Lester, a heavy sensation settled in the pit of her stomach. At the mention of marriage, he'd let go of her hand like a hot potato. Cameron was going to leave and break her heart. Again. She would dry up into a little old widow-woman who raised cats for company.

She could barely smile when Lester said his goodbyes.

"He's the same as ever," Cameron said, shaking his head as Lester faded into the crowd.

"Cameron! Hey, Cameron!"

"Oh man, Patti? Is that you?"

"Yes, it's me," she said with a laugh. "Hey, Jessie. How are you doing?" Patti reached up and kissed Cameron's cheek. "How's life treating you in Houston?"

"Good, how about you?"

"Pretty good," she said. "The kids keep me busy."

"Mama! Mama! Come here!" called a high little voice near the fire.

Patti chuckled. "See what I mean? Good to see you, Cameron. You too, Jessie."

She walked over to a little boy and took hold of his small grubby hand. She smiled at Cameron over her shoulder one more time before her son dragged her away.

"I think she loved you." Jessie's voice was a whisper. It had been difficult to stand there and witness that particular reunion. Patti was the girlfriend Cameron had broken up with right before the prom. She'd been hurt when he'd left Salt Fork. *Before* he had left, though she hadn't let on.

"She didn't really love me," Cameron said. "She was better off with Bubba anyway."

Jessie didn't know what to say. Luckily, the mayor began introducing the candidates for homecoming queen and king. She took her pad and pen from around her neck and jotted down names for her article.

"Are you okay?" Cameron asked, looking down at Jessie's bent head. She seemed quiet and withdrawn tonight.

Not looking up from her notes, Jessie nodded.

When the mayor announced their names, the young couples moved forward to stand by him. Cameron remembered how he and Patti had been voted king and queen their senior year. It hadn't meant much to him. He'd already been itching to leave, to get on with his life, to study medicine.

The band started playing the alma mater and everyone joined in. Cameron watched the shadows of the flickering flames dance across Jessie's face. He wanted her again, to bring her to fulfillment, to share the pleasure with her. Last night... words couldn't describe last night. He was scared as hell about what he was feeling. If he were smart, he would go back to Houston and forget Jessie.

She turned and smiled uncertainly. Doubt and longing shone in her eyes.

Cameron clasped his fingers around the back of her neck again and squeezed reassuringly. "Are you ready?"

Jessie nodded, unable to speak. *Ready to make love. Ready to follow you anywhere. But not ready for a broken heart.*

"Let's go, then." He propelled her away from the crowd.

Cameron's touch burned through Jessie's sweater. Rivulets of sexual awareness tingled down her spine. She wanted him to make love to her again. She wanted to store away as many memories as possible to keep her warm during the long lonely nights ahead.

The house was invitingly cozy when they entered. Jessie had left the heaters going.

"Got anything to drink?" Cameron asked, shucking out of his jacket.

"There's some bourbon. Or I could make a pot of coffee."

"Coffee sounds good." He tossed the jacket over the back of a chair, before sitting at the table.

Thankful for something to do, Jessie filled the coffee maker and plugged it in. She felt awkward. They were going to end up in bed. She knew that, even welcomed it. But she hated being so unsophisticated.

The coffee maker sputtered with familiar gurgling noises. Jessie sat at the kitchen table next to Cameron and removed the journalist's pad from around her neck. She'd taken lots of notes. Her readers would not be disappointed.

Cameron picked it up and flipped through the pages. "Get any juicy tidbits?"

Jessie laughed. "Not much happens in Salt Fork. You know that. *We* were probably the hottest topic of discussion. Or didn't you notice?"

"I noticed the old tabbies' eyes bulging with curiosity," he said. "Were their mouths hanging open because I was back, or the fact that we were together?"

Jessie went to the counter and poured the coffee. "Probably both. You've stayed away a long time. Coming back twice in two months is a miracle in itself." She handed him a steaming mug before sitting down again.

He took a sip and watched her. "And the fact that we were together?"

She nearly choked on the hot coffee. The sensual tone of his voice shot tiny jolts of desire straight down to her core. She realized she had never believed they would really get together. Jessie took another drink to clear her throat and thoughts. "That's another miracle, isn't it?"

"How so?"

Jessie fidgeted with the notepad, opening and closing

it, trying to hide the trembling in her fingers. This was not the time to discuss their relationship. *Because they had no relationship.* "I usually go to these events by myself. The fact that you and I were together... Everyone will think–" She shrugged. *She* knew what everyone would think. Did Cameron care that his name would be coupled with hers? No, of course not.

"What would everyone think?" he said quietly. "That we're an item? Lester certainly thought so, didn't he?"

His eyes smoldered with an intensity that left Jessie shaking. She'd always known she was out of her league in her dealings with Cameron. She wasn't sure what he wanted from her now.

"Lester was always a fool," she said. Pushing away from the table, she stuffed the notepad in her purse, then went to the sink and poured the rest of her coffee down the drain. She gripped the edge of the counter for support and tried not to think how foolish she was acting. Wishing for the moon, wanting Cameron forever and ever. She dashed a hand across her eyes and desperately held back a sniff. She refused to let Cameron see just how unsophisticated she really was.

"Jess?" The voice was low, seductive. Cameron whispered it in her ear, bracing his arms on either side of her, imprisoning her between his warm body and the cold kitchen counter. His breath scorched her ear and she tilted her head back. Swallowing the lump of tears in her throat, Jessie made a decision. For this one night, she would forget he was going to leave. She would pretend they were forever and ever. And afterwards? She refused to think about that.

* * *

"Jess, wake up." Cameron kissed the silky hollow at the base of her throat. His hand kneaded one firm breast. "Wake up, sweetheart. It's late. I need to get back to the ranch." He pulled on his slacks, then groped in the dark for his socks.

Jessie rolled over and yawned. She glanced at the clock on the nightstand where the orange numerals glowed: *two-thirty*. She stretched, and then snuggled deeper under the covers. "Why don't you stay the night?"

She watched Cameron sit on the edge of the bed, his back to her. A very sexy back. He didn't say anything. The tendons in his shoulders tightened. *He doesn't want to stay. He's leaving.* She reached one hand from under the quilts and rubbed the corded muscles.

Cameron bowed his shoulders. The muscles flexed beneath her fingers. "That feels good," he said, his voice a low growl.

Jessie pushed the covers away and knelt behind him. She massaged the tendons until they relaxed. Goosebumps spread across his skin as her nails raked up and down his spine.

As swift as a panther, he turned and captured her hands, raised them above her head and pushed her down into the mattress. All it took was a touch or a look and the desire between them ignited. It had never been like this with TR. Jessie quickly blocked that thought from her mind.

"Again?" she asked, arching upward, inviting his caress, smiling at the man who had stolen her heart so long ago.

"Again," he said, grinding his mouth to hers.

The bed squeaked in time to the rhythm of their passion. After the fires were banked, they lay together in the darkness still joined.

"I really should go, Jess," he said in her ear.

"Don't you *want* to stay?"

"Damn it! Of course I want to stay. I just don't want my mother or anyone else talking about you after I'm gone."

A knot formed in the middle of Jessie's stomach. Cameron was leaving; he'd just said so. She tightened her hold around his shoulders, as if to prevent him from going. "It's a little late to protect my reputation, don't you think? Stay the night with me. Please?"

Cameron kissed her forehead, then her lips. She felt good in his arms. No woman had ever fit him so perfectly. There was something definitely special about Jessie. But that thought was dangerous. Long-term relationships and marriage weren't in his plans yet. *Marriage, whoa! Where had that come from?*

The look in Jessie's eyes melted something in him. Hell, it was only one night. He started to move inside her again. "I'll stay, Jess. I'll stay."

It was close to noon when Jessie woke up. Brilliant sunlight streamed through the windows, causing her to blink back the sleep from her eyes. A sense of well-being permeated her soul. Her body was replete, but her stomach rumbled with hunger. It had been a long night. A glorious, wonderful, long night. She smiled and turned over to reach for Cameron.

He was gone.

The excruciating wrench in her gut almost made her sick. A tight fist clutched at her heart. She willed herself to calm down. Cameron had left without saying goodbye. Again. Jessie's contentment vanished, replaced with a feeling of abandonment and heartache. She took a deep breath, then another... and then sniffed the air.

Was that coffee she smelled?

Throwing back the covers, she jumped out of bed and dashed to the kitchen, only to stop short in the middle of the hallway when she realized she was naked. Good lord, she never slept naked. She'd never been able to sleep without clothes. Until last night. But then, there hadn't been much sleep going on last night. Jessie walked back to her room, slipped on a robe and tightened the belt on the way to the kitchen.

At the door, she peeked in and saw Cameron sitting at the table with Katnip on his lap. The old tomcat purred as the strong hands rubbed and petted him. Magic hands, Jessie thought. They made her want to purr, too.

"Good morning, sleepyhead." Cameron flashed a grin that curled her toes. At the same time, she felt vulnerable, naked under the robe. She adjusted the belt more securely.

"A little late for modesty, don't you think?" Cameron asked with a wink.

"Force of habit," Jessie said. Blushing, she hurried to the counter and poured a cup of coffee. *Cameron hadn't left.* In fact, he looked right at home, sitting at her kitchen table with Katnip on his lap. Did he look that way when he was standing at an operating table? Probably more so. He had rejected rural living and turned his back on the ranch and Salt Fork.

"Why so quiet, Jess?"

She sat across from him at the table. "Tired, I guess."

"A good kind of tired, I hope." Again, that killer smile.

"Yes, a good kind of tired." She sipped her coffee and lost herself in the sensual warmth of Cameron's gaze. His eyes were deadlier than his smile.

Suddenly, her stomach growled.

"Hungry?" he asked.

She nodded. "What do you want for breakfast?"

"You. I can't seem to get enough of you."

Her lungs collapsed, refusing to function normally. The low intimacy of his voice, the intensity of his stare, shattered her nerve endings. Her stomach rumbled again.

Cameron laughed. "I think we better get something to eat. We used a lot of calories last night and you don't have many reserves."

Jessie jumped up, opened the refrigerator and rummaged around, trying to ignore the quiver in her stomach that had nothing to do with lack of food. "You think I'm too skinny? Is that what you're trying to tell me?" She stared at the meager contents on the glass shelves. She needed to go grocery shopping. She needed... *oh my.*

Cameron pulled her away from the fridge and into his arms, kicking the refrigerator door closed. "I don't think you're too skinny. I think you're perfect. Beautiful. Sexy."

"You think I'm sexy?" Jessie leaned her head on his shoulder, breathing in his clean masculine scent and feeling his steady heartbeat against her ear.

"Oh, yeah, sweetheart. I think you're damned sexy." He bent down and kissed her.

When his stomach growled, Jessie pulled away and smiled, poking a finger against the massive chest. "You're hungry too, buster. Don't deny it. Can't live on love alone, you know."

Cameron picked her up and carried her to the bedroom. "We can try, can't we?"

"Put me down," she protested, laughing as she flung her arms around his neck. "We need food. I'm starving."

He let her slide to the floor. Her body rubbed slowly against his. The erotic friction caused her robe to come undone.

"Let's go to the cafe for breakfast, brunch or whatever." Cameron slipped the robe from her shoulders and kissed her, caressing her breasts with gentle fingers. "But first, let's take a shower and get dressed."

"A shower? As in, together?" Jessie floated on a sea of sensation as his hands worked their magic over her body. Anticipation ignited a fire in her veins.

"Definitely together," Cameron said, as he steered her toward the bathroom door.

CHAPTER NINE

"*I* can't eat another bite." Jessie pushed her plate away and wiped her mouth. She watched Cameron sop a fluffy biscuit in Sarah Sue's famous cream gravy. He glanced at her and winked. Jessie's heart flip-flopped. The love she felt for him burst the seams of her heart. Their time together was precious. Would Cameron miss her after he left?

Sarah Sue walked up and refilled their coffee cups. "Y'all want any dessert?"

"None for me, thanks," Jessie said.

The waitress put her hand on her hip and frowned.

"Something wrong?" Cameron asked, throwing down his napkin and glancing at Jessie.

"Well now, I was just wondering why Jessie is here instead of over at the football field."

"Oh my gosh!" Jessie said. "I completely forgot."

Cameron looked from her to Sarah Sue. "Forgot

what?"

"Why darlin', you *have* been away too long." She shook her finger in his face. "It's *homecoming*. You know? The Big Game. This afternoon. Three o'clock?"

Jessie shoved away from the table. "What time is it?" she asked Cameron.

"Almost two. Why?"

"I'll tell you why," the waitress said. "Jessie is one of Salt Fork's best feature writers. She interviews the coaches and players and writes a real nice column about the game. I always look forward to reading it." She set the coffee pot down and totaled up the bill. "It's surprising Jessie forgot. Never has before. Maybe she had other things on her mind." She handed the bill to Cameron. "Not that I don't think it's great you two are spending time together–"

"Sarah Sue, thanks for reminding me." Jessie felt a blush stain her cheeks. Her friend was notorious for minding other people's business. She turned to Cameron. "I really need to get over to the stadium. How could you forget? You came back for homecoming, didn't you?"

Sarah Sue snorted. "Of course, he didn't come back for homecoming, darlin'. Never bothered coming before. Any blind fool knows why he's here."

Jessie's cheeks grew redder. She turned and walked quickly out the door.

Cameron took care of the bill. He tucked an extra twenty in Sarah Sue's pocket and kissed her cheek. "Thanks. I think."

"Always like to help people dear to me. And Jessie's

– 157 –

very dear. You two make a mighty fine couple. Don't go breaking her heart again, you hear?"

"Again?"

Sarah Sue grabbed the coffee pot. "Never mind, darlin'. Go on now, Jessie's waiting."

Cameron turned to leave.

"You're a fool if you let her get away, Cameron McCade," she called when he reached the door.

"I know it," he said over his shoulder.

"Know what?" Jessie stood just outside the entrance.

He took her elbow and led her to the car. "That I'm a fool." He placed a finger on her mouth. "Don't ask. Let's get to the stadium."

The bleachers were almost packed when they pulled into the parking lot. Jessie tied her notepad around her neck. "You get the seats while I do the interviews. I like to sit up high. Fifty-yard line."

Cameron smiled. "So you can see the whole field?"

"Exactly. You wouldn't be making fun of me again, would you?" she asked. "I know this isn't as exciting as a professional game, but it's important to people around here. It used to be important to you, too."

She opened the door and climbed out. Cameron leaned over the console and stared up at her. "Hey, Jess?"

Turning back, she bent to look at him, a question in her eyes.

"I love it when you throw my past in my face. Don't ever change." He brushed a finger against the soft skin of her cheek.

"You said that to me once before," she said.

"Did I? When?"

She straightened and dug a pen from the bottom of her purse. "You figure it out, Cameron." Jessie closed the door and disappeared through the gates leading to the football field.

Cameron engaged the alarm system on his car. The Jag looked out of place in the middle of all the pickups and farm vehicles. Just as he felt out of place, had *always* felt out of place. Except for this visit. This visit was different somehow what with seeing Jess and making love to her. What the hell was he going to do about her?

At the ticket booth, he slapped some bills down, his mind on Jessie. "Two, please."

"Hey, Cameron." Patti Garrison smiled through the glass enclosure. "If one of these is for Jessie, I know just where she likes to sit."

"You sell tickets often?" He shoved the money under the window.

"Every game." She counted change and handed him the tickets. "My oldest is on the team, and Bubba's head coach."

"Bubba's the coach?" Cameron took the tickets from her. She sounded so proud and content.

"Sure is," Patti said. "They hired him after he graduated from Tech. We married while we were both at college and decided to come back home so we could raise our kids in Salt Fork."

"And you're happy here?" Cameron asked.

She shrugged. "As happy as one might expect, I guess. I didn't think so at the time, but breaking up with you was one of the best things that could have happened. I have a good husband and five great kids. And I enjoy living in Salt Fork."

"I thought... Jessie said..." Cameron shook his head, trying to straighten out his confused thoughts.

"I know what Jessie must think." Patti leaned forward and looked him in the eye. "But believe me, it wasn't *my* heart that was broken when you left town."

He gripped the tickets in his hand. "What do you mean by that?"

Patti moved back. "Nothing. Forget it. Enjoy the game. Your mom and Tyler are already up in the stands. Austin and Kelsey, too. Dallas better hurry or he'll miss the kickoff. Nice seeing you, Cameron. I've got tickets to sell, and there's a long line behind you."

He glanced over his shoulder and stepped away from the booth. Patti's words disturbed him. Sarah Sue's warning replayed in his mind. Both women seemed to think he had broken Jessie's heart when he'd left town. But how could that be? They had barely known each other back in high school. He'd been aware of her crush on him, but it certainly hadn't been strong enough to warrant a broken heart.

Pushing through the crowd, Cameron slowly made his way to the grandstand, stopping to exchange greetings with old friends. Small town friendliness, Jessie would say. It wasn't so bad. He must be getting soft–or *old*. Or maybe Jessie was getting to him. Yeah, Jessie was definitely getting to him.

"Hey, Cameron! Up here."

Shading his eyes against the blinding afternoon sun,

Cameron searched the crowded bleachers. High up in the stands, he spotted his two brothers, Tyler and Austin, sitting with his mom. A quick glance at his ticket stubs told him all he needed to know. He took the steps two at a time.

"Well, well. Isn't this cozy?" he said. He hadn't expected to share his date with his family.

Austin slapped him on the shoulder and grinned. "Isn't it, though?"

Ruth pulled Cameron down onto the seat next to her. "Sit down, Cam. It's not what you think. We always sit up here at the games. The view's great, and it's fun watching Jessie jot down notes for her stories." She buttoned the collar of her jacket and looked at the cheerleaders down below. "You didn't come home last night."

"No," he said, feeling like he was sixteen again.

"Jessie's a good girl. I don't want to see her get hurt."

"No one's going to get hurt, Mom." Everyone thought he was a heartbreaker, even his mother.

"You don't know that," Ruth said. "I told you she cares for you. If you spend the night at her place and then just go back to Houston–" She shook her head. "I'll never understand these modern ways. It wasn't like this when your father and I were young."

"Times change," Cameron said.

"*People* don't change."

"Let up, Ma," Tyler said, rolling his eyes at his brother.

"Hey, Grams!" Kelsey ran up the steps toward them

with a snack tray loaded with sodas, popcorn and nachos. "They were out of Spanish peanuts, so I got cashews instead. If you don't want them, I'll eat 'em." She climbed over the bleachers, dodging people right and left, concentrating on balancing the tray and getting to her seat.

"Here, let me help you." Austin took the tray from his daughter.

"Thanks," she said and flopped down beside him. Leaning around, she smiled at Cameron. "I saw Jessie, Uncle Cam. She'll be here in a minute." Kelsey waved to someone sitting lower in the stands. "There's my teacher, Miss Rogers. She's so cool. I'm going to say hello to her." She jumped up and was gone in a flash.

"Does she ever stay in one place for more than a minute?" Cameron asked, watching his niece down below.

Austin shook his head and grinned. "No, she's a ten-year-old whirlwind that never stops."

Cameron eased a cramp in one of his legs. "I wonder what's keeping Dallas?"

"I don't know," Tyler said. "He left the house at dawn. I took Ma to Abilene this morning, then came straight here. Something must have come up. He'll be here, though. He never misses a game."

Ruth set her bag of popcorn on her lap. "Did you see Patti?" she asked Cameron.

He looked at her out of the corner of his eye. "Yeah, I saw her at the bonfire last night and at the ticket booth just a minute ago."

Ruth let out a long sigh. "Her son is on the varsity

team. I wish I had a grandson on the team. I wish I had a grandson, period. Or another granddaughter or two." She sighed again.

"Don't start that again," Cameron said. "You'll have more grandkids one of these days."

Austin put his arm around Ruth's shoulders. "Maybe Kelsey will try out for the team when she gets to high school. She's a fine little athlete."

"But she's a girl!" Ruth said. "Don't you dare go putting such notions into that child's head. Soccer is bad enough. Football is too rough for a girl."

"Oh, I don't know about that," Austin said. "Kelsey has a lot of speed. She'd make a darn good running back."

"Who'd make a good running back?" Jessie asked, scooting past Cameron and sitting between him and Ruth. She handed him a cup of hot cocoa.

"Oh, Jessie," Ruth cried. "Austin wants Kelsey to play football!"

Jessie patted Ruth's hand. "He's just teasing you, I'm sure." She frowned at Austin, then winked at Cameron.

"How'd the interviews go?" Cameron blew the cocoa before taking a sip. He hadn't realized Jessie was so close to his family. Close enough to soothe his mother's feelings and scold Austin in the same breath. He'd known she was on friendly terms with them; she'd been invited to Ruth's birthday party. But he'd been too busy that day to see her interact with any of them.

"The interviews went great," Jessie said, warming her fingers on her cocoa cup. "Bubba says there's a slim chance we might win today."

"Only a slim chance?" Cameron asked.

Jessie nodded. "The team hasn't had a successful season this year. Things are different than when we were kids and you were playing."

Everything seemed to be different since they were kids, Cameron thought. Or was it the same? His attraction to Jessie had been strong back then. His feelings for her now were getting completely out of hand. "What's their record?"

"They've won one and lost six," she said, sipping her cocoa and gazing around the stands.

"Damn." Times *had* changed. Salt Fork had made it to the play-offs his junior and senior year.

Kelsey climbed over everyone's legs to return to her seat and grabbed her plate of nachos and took a bite, then licked the gooey cheese from her fingers.

"Kelsey, don't lick your fingers," Ruth scolded. "Where are your manners?" She handed her granddaughter a paper napkin.

"Aw, Grams."

"Don't 'aw, Grams' me, young lady." Ruth smiled and gave her a quick hug. "They're raising the flag. Now watch those nachos and don't spill anything when you stand up."

The band played the national anthem. Not many people sang along, but a familiar voice, slightly off-key, belted out the words to "The Star Spangled Banner". Cameron turned toward the voice. Sure enough it was old Mr. Butler. He'd always sung loudly at the games when Cameron was on the team.

The eerie sensation of being caught in a time warp wove its ghostly fingers around him. The same strangling feelings he'd felt as a kid enveloped him now, stifling and smothering him. He broke out in a cold sweat.

Jessie laid her fingers on his arm, squeezed, comforted. Something in her eyes and her touch calmed the turmoil roiling inside before it almost devoured him.

"Are you okay?" she asked.

Cameron forced himself to smile. He stroked her hand still lying on his arm, thankful for the serenity she'd bestowed on him. "Sure. I'm okay." *Now.*

He sipped his hot chocolate and tried not to think about Jessie sitting close beside him. He especially tried not to think about her calming effect on his restless soul. Could Jess be the cure he'd been seeking for so long?

When she crossed her legs, her thigh brushed against his, and desire tugged low in Cameron's stomach. Visions of smooth bare legs tangling with his made his heart pound. His feelings for Jessie were definitely getting out of hand. He'd been aware of all sorts of strange emotions since he'd been home, emotions he'd rather live without.

At half time, Jessie pointed to the gates. "Look, they're bringing in the homecoming candidates." She opened her pad and scratched some notes as four classic convertibles snaked along the paved track surrounding the football field. Four girls and four boys waved to the crowds.

Once again, time rolled back as Cameron saw himself riding in one of those cars with Patti. The feelings of being trapped and suffocated rose within him again.

Jessie looked at him and smiled, her eyes holding a promise of passion and something more. Cameron took a deep cleansing breath and smiled back. He was at a crossroads in his life and didn't have a plan or a clue. The only thing he knew was somehow, some way, Jessie played an important part in his future.

The Bulldogs are going for the field goal with seven seconds left in the game. Randy Garrison runs, kicks it high... and it's good! Salt Fork wins: 17-14! The voice over the loudspeaker reverberated with excitement as the fans in the seats went wild.

"We won! We won!" Kelsey screamed, jumping up and down, spilling popcorn all over the place.

Jessie cheered at the top of her lungs and turned to hug Cameron. He caught her to him and squeezed her tight. Tilting her head back, she laughed with joy. It felt so good and so right to be in Cameron's arms, but something was wrong, she could sense it.

"You two are getting mighty lovey-dovey," Ruth said.

Jessie blushed as Cameron quickly set her away from him. She hurriedly scribbled some last minute notes for her story, trying to ignore the abandoned feeling in the pit of her stomach. He was already distancing himself from her. She swallowed a sob as she collected her things and stuffed them in her bag.

Her notepad dropped to the ground and Ruth bent to pick it up. "I wonder why Dallas never showed up?" She handed the pad to Jessie.

"I don't know," Austin said, gathering the empty cups and scattered wrappers. "He's really going to be sorry he missed the game."

Kelsey stood on the bleachers, watching the crowd, waving to friends. "Are you taking Jessie to the dance tonight, Uncle Cam?"

"I'm not sure..." He stared at Jessie in a strange way.

She felt tension radiating from Cameron's body, a different kind of tension. Was he having regrets? About coming back, wanting her, making love to her? He was backing off; he didn't want a relationship with her because she didn't fit in with his plans. She never had.

"Hey," Kelsey said, standing on tiptoes, craning her neck for a better look. "Uncle Dallas is coming up here."

Jessie slung her purse over her shoulder. *Great, just great.* Dallas never missed a chance to hassle her about the mineral rights. She hadn't seen him since she'd given the go ahead to lease them. She was stuck with no way to escape, surrounded by McCades.

Dallas fought his way against the crowd, and as he approached, Jessie knew something terrible must have happened. A frown etched his forehead, his lips were set in a rigid line and his eyes smoldered with anger.

Dallas McCade was an intimidating man, even in a good mood. In a towering rage–Jessie shuddered. Luckily, he had never lost his temper in their dealings together.

"Something's definitely up," Tyler said. "Dallas

looks madder than a hornet."

With the crowd finally behind him, the oldest McCade brother climbed the last few steps to where Jessie stood with his family. She wondered what had happened to make him so angry. When he fixed his eyes on her, she instinctively stepped closer to Cameron.

Dallas looked at his brother, then back at Jessie. "It's too late to hide. I didn't think you'd really do it, Jessie. Mom trusted you, but I should have known better. You're a lying, conniving, scheming... *woman!*" He spat out the last word with scathing contempt.

Cameron took a step forward, his fists clenched by his sides. "Dallas..." he said warningly.

"What on earth is wrong with you?" Ruth cried. "Why are you talking so ugly to our sweet Jessie?"

"Our *sweet* Jessie has gone behind our backs and leased the rights on the Diamondback Ranch to Copper River Oil Company."

"That's not true!" Jessie said.

Dallas snorted with disgust. "Copper River is moving heavy equipment onto the north section of the ranch. *My* ranch, Jessie. They showed me the lease agreement. Your signature is on it."

Jessie bit her lip. "I know. I signed it. But I didn't do it behind your back. I told Ruth–"

"Oh, dear," Ruth said, sitting down again.

Dallas' jaw dropped. "You told Mom, but didn't tell me?"

Cameron put his arm around Jessie's shoulder. "She told me, too."

"And no one bothered to tell me?" Dallas yelled. "To

warn me?"

Jessie looked at Ruth. "You said you would tell Dallas. Why didn't you?"

Tears gathered in Ruth's eyes. She wiped her nose on a napkin. "I didn't think anything would happen so soon. I put off telling him, because I knew he'd be upset. And with Cameron coming back for homecoming... I knew he was coming back to see you, Jessie. I didn't want to spoil things for you two."

Jessie faced Dallas again. "I'm sorry. I know I promised not to lease the mineral rights, but I was going to lose the garage. There was no other way."

"There's always another way, Jess." Dallas settled his Stetson on his head, turned his back on her, and stalked down the stadium steps.

Ruth stood up. "I want to go home," she said, her voice sounding old and fragile.

"Ruth, I'm sorry. I should have told Dallas myself," Jessie cried. "I didn't mean for any of this to happen. I know how all of you feel about drilling on your land. I didn't mean to hurt you."

Ruth blew her nose on the napkin again. "Oh, Jessie. I know you didn't. But Dallas is so angry..." She patted Jessie's forearm. "We'll talk later. I need to get on home."

She hurried down the concrete steps. Tyler and Austin followed, with Kelsey trailing behind.

Jessie was left alone with Cameron. He was watching the cheerleaders down on the field, making a human pyramid to celebrate the victory.

"Thanks for standing up for me," she said.

He didn't turn to face her, but kept staring down at the cheerleaders on the field. "Jess, I ... Damn!"

An audible gasp rose from the crowds milling around in the stands.

Jessie gripped his arm. ""Oh my God! They've fallen!"

The girl who'd been on top lay still on the ground. The other cheerleaders gathered around her.

"Cameron, you have to do something," Jessie said. "The ambulance has already left the stadium."

"Come on!" He grabbed Jessie's hand and ran down the concrete steps. Vaulting over the chain link fence, he left Jessie to follow any which way she could.

CHAPTER TEN

Cameron sat in the back of Gussie Ferguson's Florist Shop delivery van with Hilda Vandeford lying on the makeshift stretcher. The girl's mother sat across from him holding her daughter's hand. Mayor Vandeford was at the wheel, with Gussie riding shotgun.

As soon as he'd reached the fallen cheerleader, Cameron had gone into doctor mode, issuing orders, focusing on what he could do to stabilize the injured girl. She'd tumbled from the top of the human pyramid and landed in a crumpled heap. Luckily, she'd only suffered a broken wrist and collarbone. Maybe a slight concussion.

It could have been worse. Much worse.

The interior of the van was dark except for the headlights streaming in from the back windows. Jessie was following in Cameron's car. She'd wanted to ride in the van, but there wasn't room and they'd need his Jag to return to Salt Fork.

"Is she going to be all right?" Mrs. Vandeford asked for the hundredth time. He couldn't blame her. She was worried about her daughter.

He leaned over Hilda and examined her eyes one more time, looking for signs of concussion. "I believe she'll be fine once she gets the broken bones set."

The girl groaned and tried to adjust her position on the stretcher. "Oh, Mama–"

"Shh, honey," said her mother. "We're almost to the hospital."

"I hurt... all over."

"I know, but Dr. McCade's here. You're going to be fine." Mrs. Vandeford smiled tremulously at Cameron. "Thank goodness, you were in the stands. I don't know what we would have done if you hadn't been there."

"I'm glad I could help."

The woman smoothed her daughter's forehead, wiping wisps of hair back in place. "I wish they'd hurry up and find a doctor for the new clinic." She hesitated. "I don't know you, but I've heard about you. Small town gossip, you know. Have you thought about–oh, my."

She gripped the edge of her seat as the van lurched to a stop. The mayor jumped out and came around to open the back doors. "We're here."

"Finally," his wife said in relief.

Cameron climbed out and stepped back as two orderlies in green scrubs rushed out of the emergency room to help remove the patient from the vehicle. He quickly told them what had happened and the extent of the injuries, then watched as they whisked Hilda into the hospital, her mother by her side.

Mayor Vandeford stayed behind to shake Cameron's hand. "I can't thank you enough, Dr. McCade. You saved my daughter's life–"

"It wasn't that bad–"

"No, thank God, but it could have been. I don't know if you're aware, but Salt Fork is in dire need of a competent, dedicated doctor. Jessie Devine has worked to get the new clinic built, but we're still looking for a doctor. I know Jessie was meaning to ask you to fill the position. I hope you will seriously consider the offer."

"I don't know..."

"Think about it," the mayor said. "I came to live in Salt Fork after you left town, so I don't know you personally, but I know your family. The job is yours, if you want it."

Cameron didn't know what to say. His first impulse was to say yes. But he wasn't used to acting on impulse. He was acting on gut instinct where Jess was concerned and it was proving to be a wild ride. His life and career needed to be carefully planned and thought out. He'd always planned everything carefully in the past.

And look where it's gotten you.

Out of the corner of his eye, he saw Jessie hurrying toward him from the parking lot. That calmness only she could provide settled in his stomach.

For years, he'd been living according to his well-thought out plans. But he wasn't happy or content. He lead a hectic life, he was nursing an ulcer and he'd become someone he didn't even like. And worst of all, he'd never conquered the damned restlessness that had dogged his every step.

"Dr. McCade," the mayor said, "I have to go see about my daughter. Thank you again. Please consider the clinic. Salt Fork needs you." He turned toward the automatic glass doors leading to the emergency room.

To hell with planning. "Wait a minute," Cameron said.

The mayor turned toward him. "Yes?"

It was now or never. "I'll take the job."

The mayor beamed a smile and walked back to shake his hand. "Thank you, Dr. McCade. Thank you so much. Welcome back to Salt Fork."

Jessie crossed the street just as the mayor entered the emergency room. She was out of breath, her cheeks glowing from the cold wind. She looked beautiful.

In that moment, Cameron knew he'd made the right decision.

"Is Hilda going to be okay?" she asked as soon as she reached his side.

Cameron pulled her into his arms and kissed her hard. She felt so good, smelled so sweet, and tasted oh so wonderful.

Jessie laughed. "I take it, she's going to fine?"

"Yes, I think so."

"I'm glad. You were great back there. Taking control of the situation, making sure Hilda wasn't dangerously injured. I know the mayor and his wife are thankful you were at the game and able to help."

"That's my job, Jess. Helping people."

"But not every person would have acted so quickly. It was something to see you in action. I can tell you're an excellent doctor."

Cameron smiled. "Well, thank you, sweetheart. I enjoy helping people. It's very satisfying. Exhausting, but satisfying."

"You wouldn't have it any other way, would you?"

"No, I wouldn't." Cameron hugged her close and twirled around, capturing her lips in another soul-searing kiss. He'd never get tired of kissing Jessie. Never. And now, they'd have a chance to see where their relationship would take them. They'd have time to explore the volatile chemistry they shared.

Jessie pulled back. "Not that I'm complaining, but this isn't exactly a private place to be doing this."

Cameron hugged her again. "We're celebrating."

"Oh? What's the occasion?"

Cameron set her from him and made a little bow. For the first time in his life he felt carefree and content. "Congratulate me, sweetheart. You're looking at Salt Fork's new resident physician."

Jessie's jaw dropped. *"What?"*

"Mayor Vandeford asked me if I wanted to move my practice to Salt Fork. I told him yes. He said you were meaning to ask me. So why didn't you?"

Jessie looked shell-shocked. "But I did. I asked you that first night when your car broke down and I drove you to the ranch. You told me you had no intention of moving back to Salt Fork–"

"Well, I changed my mind."

"But what about your plans? What about that big promotion?"

"I declined the promotion when I went back to

Houston. It didn't feel right."

"And this does?" she asked, searching his face. She was so dear to him. Why hadn't he realized it before?

He took her hand in his. "This feels very right. A couple of nights ago up on Lover's Point, you and I started over. Now, I'm starting over with my career."

Jess removed her hand from his grasp. "Are you sure you want to do this, Cameron? It's such a drastic change. Have you thought it through?"

He shrugged. "Only to a certain degree. I thought I had everything I wanted in Houston. But something was lacking, Jess. And I realized I missed Salt Fork and the ranch." *And you*. But now wasn't the time to tell her that. Their relationship was still too fragile. Cameron didn't want anything to rock the boat.

"You can't just leave Houston and your practice. That's all you ever wanted. You couldn't wait to leave Salt Fork when you were a kid. And you rarely came back to visit."

"I know. But some of that was because I've been too damned busy to visit. Med school was brutal; my residency even more so. Besides, what does an eighteen-year-old know about life? How many kids that age know what they really want?"

Again, she searched his face as if trying to read his soul. "You always seemed to know what you wanted."

"I made a wrong turn somewhere along the line." And he'd just figured out where that wrong turn had been.

Jessie took a deep breath. "So, you're really coming back? Where will you live?"

Cameron took her in his arms again. "I'll stay at the ranch, at first. Then you can help me find a house in town. I'll need to live close to the clinic."

"The clinic," she said. "I can't believe you're going to actually work at the clinic."

It was his turn to search her face. Something didn't seem quite right. "You haven't congratulated me, Jess. Don't you want me to move back?"

Jessie looped her arms around his neck and smiled, but it looked forced to Cameron. "Of course. If it's what you really want."

"I really want."

"Then congratulations, Cameron."

He kissed her and for a split second, she hesitated before melting under his onslaught. He would have to figure out what was wrong, but now that he was moving back to Salt Fork, he would have plenty of time to devote to Jessie.

He could hardly wait.

"So, darlin', I don't understand why you're moping around like this." Sarah Sue wiped the Formica countertop with a sponge. Jessie sat on one of the stools, drinking a cup of coffee. It was late and the diner was closed. Oftentimes, Jessie came to Sarah Sue's Café after she'd closed up shop to visit and gossip, share a little girl-talk.

"I know Cameron's been gone a week, but he's coming back," Sarah Sue said. "And he's coming back for good. You should be in tall cotton, what with him moving his practice to Salt Fork. Your wish has finally come true. And you told me yourself, you wished he'd work in that clinic of yours. That wish has come true, too."

Jessie stirred more sugar into the cup. "I don't know what's wrong with me. I should be overjoyed. And you're right; I have wished that Cameron would return and want to take up where we left off all those years ago. So what the hell is the matter with me?"

"You're gun-shy, that's what you are," said Sarah Sue. "And who could blame you? Cameron hurt you when he left to go to college. But you've been given another chance. Go for it, girl."

Jessie sipped her coffee. Going to the prom with Cameron had been a major turning point in her life. Up on Lover's Point, he'd awakened her to passion and desire. Given her a taste of what it could be like between a man and a woman. *Between them*. He'd been kind and gentle. She'd been so young and inexperienced.

She remembered being scared, too. Sitting in the parked truck alone with Cameron McCade...

"Earth to Jessie." Sarah Sue waved the coffee pot under Jessie's nose, jolting her from her thoughts.

"Sorry." She took another sip of coffee. It was cold. Just like she had felt after the prom when Cameron had left her on the doorstep and walked out of her life.

"Let me freshen your coffee for you," Sarah Sue said.

"Sure."

"Where'd you go? You were as far away as the man

in the moon."

"Just thinking."

"About Cameron?"

"What else?"

"Seems to me, you've been thinking about that man your whole life."

Jessie stared at the dark fragrant liquid in her cup and nodded.

Sarah Sue set the coffee pot down and picked up her sponge again. "Well, the good Lord has seen fit to give you and Cameron another chance. Just like He gave TR another chance with you."

Jessie's head snapped up. "What do you mean by that? I wasn't TR's second chance."

"Sure you were, darlin'. TR lost Dolly Mae in the prime of his life. Then he married you, didn't he?"

"Yes, but I wasn't a very good wife." TR had deserved better, no getting around that fact.

"You made him happy, Jessie. He told me so himself."

"He did? When? Where?"

"Right here. He was sitting on that very same stool you're sitting on. He used to come in at closing time, same as you do. Have his cup of coffee and piece of pie. I may not be a bartender or a psychologist, but people tend to tell me their trials and tribulations."

Jessie couldn't believe what she was hearing. "What did TR tell you?"

"Well, now. He was afraid to marry you because he knew he didn't love you like he loved his Dolly Mae. Didn't think it'd be fair to you."

Good lord. TR had thought that? "He never said anything–"

"Of course, not. He knew you didn't love him that way either."

That was the god-awful-truth, and the guilt had been killing her. Jessie cupped her hands around her mug. "I know I didn't love him as I should have. I married him without giving him my heart. But I learned to love him. It was just different, that's all." Maybe if she kept telling herself that, she might start believing it.

Sarah Sue smiled. "Sure you loved him. Everybody loved him. TR Devine was a good man."

"Yes, he was," Jessie said. "But I still don't think I was a very good wife. I failed him, Sarah Sue. I couldn't give him the child he so desperately wanted."

"That wasn't your fault. You tried, didn't you? You didn't deny him in bed, now did you?"

"No, of course not."

"There you go then. Stop beating yourself up over it. You've got yourself another chance with Cameron McCade. Don't let it slip through your fingers, darlin'."

"Just because Cameron's moving back and has agreed to practice in the medical clinic–that doesn't mean he wants to include me in his new life."

Sarah Sue almost snorted. "Yeah, right. Are you blind? That man's smitten with you. The signs are there if you just look."

"I'm not so sure." Jessie sighed. "I'll have to take it one day at a time, like always. If it happens, it happens."

"And if it doesn't," Sarah Sue said, "just enjoy it while it lasts, darlin'."

"And no regrets," Jessie said with a lift of her chin. "I'm finished living with regret and guilt. I'll do the best I can and to hell with all the rest."

Six weeks after the homecoming game, Cameron was set up at the clinic and ready for patients. He'd been living at the ranch for the past month and a half, but tonight he'd be sleeping in the house Jess had found for him two blocks from the clinic. She and his mother and brothers had spent the entire Saturday afternoon helping him move in.

Thanksgiving had come and gone. And so had Christmas. He'd been in Houston for both holidays, wishing he were back in Salt Fork. Wishing he could be with Jess.

And now he was. Life was good and looking to get better. The restlessness was gone, replaced with anticipation for the future.

"Where do you want these?" Tyler stood in the doorway leading to the living room, holding a box that looked heavy.

"What's in it?" Cameron asked. "It should be marked."

"Medical books. And I hope to God it's the last one. How many damn books you got, bro?"

"Quite a few. Here, give me it to me. These go in my bedroom."

"With pleasure."

"Quit your bellyaching–"

"Hey, Cam! Where do you want this?" Austin came up behind Tyler, carrying a big silver cooking pot.

Cameron looked at it and frowned. "That's not mine."

Ruth scooted in to stand between her two sons. "It's mine. I cooked a batch of chicken and dumplings yesterday. Put it on the stove, Austin. Dinner will be ready in fifteen minutes."

"I'll go get Jess." Cameron climbed the stairs of the old Victorian house. The place was a lot different from his loft in downtown Houston. Jess had brought over some quilts to drape over the leather furniture and she'd placed several vases of flowers on the chrome tables. Things were shaping up nicely. He felt at home here, and he liked the feeling.

Now, if only he could get things situated between himself and Jess, all would be good. Something was still not right with her. She seemed to be trying too hard, if that made any sense.

At the top of the stairs, he walked down the hall to his bedroom and stopped at the door. One wall was built entirely in shelves, and Jessie had spent the last couple of hours arranging his books. He'd tried to help her, but he was constantly being called away by his mother and brothers to oversee the placement of furniture and other stuff.

Jessie had made up his bed and he looked longingly from the lovely woman engrossed in her work to the soft bed where he wanted to take her and break in the new house in style. After dinner, he'd have to get rid of his family.

Speaking of which...

"Hey, Jess, time to wrap things up for the night. Mom's brought chicken and dumplings for dinner."

She dropped the book she was putting on the top shelf and whirled around. "Damn, you scared me."

Cameron set the box of books on the floor and closed the distance between them. "I didn't mean to scare you." He took her in his arms, loving the feel of her against his body. "Let's go downstairs and eat, then you and I can come up here for a little dessert."

Jessie held onto his shoulders and smiled. "That sounds scrumptious." She stood on tiptoes and kissed him. "Come on, I'm starved."

"Wait a minute." He tightened his hold on her and really kissed her, crushing her mouth beneath his, relishing the taste of her.

Jessie pushed out of his embrace. "Food first, buster. Lovemaking later. We've got company in the house."

"*We've?*" He liked the sound of that.

"*You* have company." She inched toward the door and smiled a provocative little smile. "Race you! Last one downstairs has to wash dishes."

She took off down the hall and Cameron didn't waste any time. He overtook her at the top of the stairs and scooped her in his arms. Jess squealed and threw her arms around his neck, laughing. He loved the sound of her laugh.

He stomped down the stairs, with a giggling armful of woman, his heart pounding, his body humming.

Tyler stepped out of the kitchen, with arms folded and a lopsided grin on his face. "If I'd known Jessie needed moving, I'd have volunteered for the job."

Cameron felt Jessie stiffen, her laughter suddenly gone. He wasn't quite sure why she'd stopped giggling, but only knew he had to do something quick.

"We were racing to the kitchen and you know how I hate to lose," Cameron said.

"Don't I, though," Tyler said, his smile widening.

Jessie wiggled in Cameron's arms and started kicking her legs. "Put me down, Cameron. Right now."

"In a minute, sweetheart. Hey, Ty, I could use your help here."

Tyler stepped forward. "At your service, Dr. McCade."

Cameron hated to let Tyler touch Jessie, but it couldn't be helped. "Here you go. Keep her a minute until I'm in the kitchen. I sure don't want to do dishes tonight."

He deposited the astonished Jessie into his brother's arms and made a production of stepping inside the kitchen. "I win!"

Jessie slid out of Tyler's grasp and marched into the kitchen, frowning mightily. "Cheater," she mumbled as she passed Cameron on the way to the table. She felt him behind her; aware of his closeness and blushed when he put his hands on her shoulders to guide her forward.

Ruth, Austin and Kelsey sat at the table. Tyler took a place near his niece. Cameron pulled a chair for Jessie, but she stood for a moment, looking at the McCade family. They were such a close-knit bunch. Except one member was conspicuously absent. He'd kept away all day long.

Jessie hated to think she'd come between Cameron and Dallas. The rancher hadn't spoken to her since the day he'd stomped up the stadium steps and told her Copper River Oil was preparing to drill on his land. He hadn't forgiven her for signing the lease papers. And he resented the fact that she and Cameron were dating.

Jessie sighed. Ever since Cameron had announced he was moving back to Salt Fork and working at the clinic, things had been getting more complicated by the minute. Oh well. All she could do was roll with the punches, and wait and see. She was good at that.

"Something sure smells good." She sat down beside Ruth, who smiled a greeting. Cameron took a seat on her left.

Ruth ladled a big helping of the dumplings in a bowl and handed it to Jessie. "Here you go, dear. Eat hearty. I know you've been working your fanny off all day long."

Kelsey held her bowl for her serving. "I've been helping, too, Grams."

"Of course, you have. Here you go, sweetie."

Ruth finished dishing out dumplings and silence descended around the table as everyone dug in and ate.

How long had Jessie wanted to be a part of a family like this? Ruth had always been like a mother to her and Jessie was glad the awkwardness of the mineral rights fiasco had faded away between them. If only Dallas could forgive and forget.

Jessie felt Cameron's knee brush hers under the table. She glanced at him and he smiled. As usual, her heart sank to her toes and the pleasant sensation of anticipation bubbled just beneath the surface of her skin.

She didn't know what the future held for her and Cameron. She'd just take one day at a time. She was good at that, too.

"There's going to be a Valentine's Dance next Friday night," Cameron told Jessie. She was helping him hang curtains in the house. The house he'd lived in for over a month now.

"Really? Where?" Jessie handed him the curtain rod. He was standing on a ladder, installing hardware.

"Over at the Rocky Hollow Club in Cactus Gap. One of my patients told me about it this afternoon. Do you want to go?"

Jessie picked up the fabric panel she'd sewn for Cameron's den. "I've never been to a Valentine's Dance."

"Well then, you're in for a treat. I'll pick you up at six, we'll grab a bite at Sarah Sue's, then head on over to Cactus Gap."

Jessie smiled as she handed him the curtain panel. "It's a date, Dr. McCade. You going to wear your Stetson?"

"Don't I always?"

"Not always." Jessie sighed and fluttered her eyelashes at him. "One of these days..."

His eyes glittered dangerously seductive. "What are you saying? You want me to wear my hat in bed?"

Jessie shrugged. "A girl can always dream, can't

she?"

Cameron climbed down from the ladder and tossed the curtain aside, amorous intent shining in his eyes as he advanced toward her.

"Hey, what are you doing? It's going to get wrinkled," Jessie cried, making a mad dash for the curtain. "I don't want to iron that sucker again."

"It'll be fine," he said, catching her arm and pulling her to him. "I'd like to make all your dreams come true, Jess."

She snuggled closer and looped her arms around his neck. "You've already made two of them come true."

Cameron nibbled her lips. "And which ones would those be?"

"You've moved back to Salt Fork and you're making my clinic a reality. I'm thankful for that. You don't know how much. I've felt so guilty about TR dying because there was no doctor close by."

"That wasn't your fault, sweetheart."

"I know, but I feel bad about TR. I wasn't a good wife. The chemistry between us was nothing compared to what you and I share."

"That wasn't your fault either," Cameron said. "You need to let go of the guilt, Jess. You were doing the best you could at the time."

"You can't know that."

He kissed her forehead and gave her a hug. "I know you. You don't do anything halfway. And you're stubborn as hell."

Jessie searched his face. "Yeah, well. Building the clinic and getting it up and running has helped me feel a little better."

"I'm glad, Jess. Now I'd like to make that other dream of yours come true."

Jessie smiled. "I'll go get your Stetson."

The doorbell rang and the look of consternation on Cameron's face made Jessie giggle.

"I wonder who that could be?" she asked.

Cameron shrugged. "Whoever it is, I'll get rid of them quick."

Jessie skipped along beside him, down the hall and down the stairs. She could see Ruth through the glass panes of the front door. "Be nice to your mother, Cameron."

He sighed. "I'm always nice to my mother. What I really want is to be nice to you." He patted her butt when he passed her on the way to the door.

"You can be nice to me later, Dr. Cowboy. I'm counting on it."

The Valentine's Dance was over, and Jessie had to admit it was the best dance she'd ever gone to–after the prom, of course. Both times she'd been Cameron's date. But she'd been his last minute choice all those years ago, no matter what he'd told her.

Tonight, she'd been his first choice. And it felt wonderful.

She leaned her head against the leather-cushioned seat of the Jag, humming one of the love songs the band had played, smiling dreamily, thinking about all the slow dances they'd shared.

The miles flew by and the lights of Salt Fork soon came into view. It took several minutes to realize Cameron hadn't turned off the road heading toward her place. He'd driven right past.

"Where are we going? I thought you were taking me home."

"I'll take you home later. We're going to Lover's Point."

"Lover's Point?"

"Yeah, there's something I want to do up there and it involves you."

She smiled hugely. "Are we going to make out?"

He chuckled, the deep sound flowing through her. "We can, if you want."

"Oh, I want."

Cameron revved the motor and the car shot up the steep incline of the bluff overlooking the canyon. He cut the motor, turned in his seat and faced Jessie.

She suddenly felt nervous, which was ridiculous. She'd come a long way from the scared fifteen-year-old she'd been that first time she'd sat parked on the bluff with Cameron.

"I would have thought there'd be more cars up here on Valentine's night," she said, looking around.

"Lucky for me, we have the place to ourselves."

He leaned across the console and took her hand in his. He kissed her knuckles and her palm. "I brought you up here because this was where we first kissed. It's also where we started over last October. You remember?"

Jessie nodded. "I remember."

"I've fallen in love with you, Jess. I think I fell in love with you the first time we parked up here after the prom, but I was too set on carrying out my plans to stop and realize it."

"Cameron, I–"

He put his fingers over her lips. "Let me finish, sweetheart. I know you had a crush on me when we were kids. I'm hoping it's grown into something more. I'm hoping you feel the same for me as I feel for you now." He fished in his sports coat pocket, drew out a square jeweler's box of black velvet and opened it.

Jessie gasped when she saw the large diamond ring glittering in the moonlight that was spilling through the windshield of the Jag. "Oh my..."

Cameron took her left hand in his and pulled her close, laying her palm on his chest. She felt the steady beat of his heart and the heat of his skin beneath the smooth fabric of his shirt.

"Jess, I love you like I never thought I could love anyone. I want you to be my wife, share my life and have my babies."

A tear slid down Jessie's cheek and she bit her lip. This is what she'd dreamed of ever since she could remember. Her most precious wish was coming true.

But it was too late.

How could she marry Cameron now? She'd broken up his tight-knit family. She had come between him and Dallas. Ruth might say Dallas would come around, but Jessie didn't put much faith in the statement. Dallas McCade was a man who held a grudge.

And what about children? Children she would never

be able to give Cameron. Children he so obviously wanted and took for granted she could give him.

Jessie still felt remorse about not giving TR a baby. How much worse would she feel, not being able to give Cameron a child? A child, Jessie suddenly realized, she wanted very badly.

"Jess? You haven't answered. I'm asking you to marry me."

Jessie took a deep fortifying breath. Would she regret turning down Cameron's offer? You bet, but the alternative seemed far worse. Besides, she was used to living with regret. And she was used to living without Cameron in her life. She'd been doing it for the last seventeen years. She could keep on doing it.

Shaking her head, Jessie tried not to cry. "I'm sorry, Cameron. But I can't marry you."

CHAPTER ELEVEN

Cameron went through the motions of seeing patients, looking down throats and into ears, listening to heartbeats and lungs, writing out prescriptions, but his mind wasn't on the work. He kept berating himself for springing the marriage proposal on Jessie too soon.

That's what came from not thoroughly planning things out. Oh, he'd planned to take her to Lover's Point and he'd bought the ring. But he hadn't taken her feelings into consideration. He'd thought she loved him, but now he realized she'd never actually said the words.

Well, neither had he, before Friday night. But that didn't change the fact that he *did* love her. And she loved him, too. There was no way she could respond to his kisses and lovemaking so deeply if she didn't love him.

Cameron made notes on a patient's chart and gave it to the nurse. He walked to his office and closed the door.

Sitting at his desk, he gazed out the window at the reddish brown fields stretching almost to the horizon.

He was glad he'd moved his practice to Salt Fork, and he enjoyed living in the house in the middle of town. But it all felt hollow and empty, because he'd pictured Jessie at his side every step of the way.

Never in a million years had he imagined a refusal when he'd asked her to marry him. They'd gotten along so well; not only in bed, but in every little way as well. He didn't remember the drive back to her house that night. He'd been in a state of shock.

He shook his head. Valentine's Day would never be the same for him. Not if he took Jessie's refusal seriously. Why had his proposal backfired? Something was going on in that stubborn brain of hers. Something keeping her from taking what Cameron was offering. It had something to do with TR Devine, he was sure of that.

Acting on impulse could only get a man so far. Especially a man who'd planned every little detail of his life up to now. Cameron decided it was time to make a few new plans. Comprehensive plans, if he wanted to convince Jessie they belonged together.

And he'd never wanted anything so badly that he could remember. He smiled when he spotted a robin on the brown lawn outside the clinic window. A sign of spring and rebirth. A new beginning.

Oh yeah. It was time to make new plans and put them into action.

* * *

The pounding in Jessie's head woke her from a restless sleep. Slowly, she opened one eye and peeked at the clock on her nightstand. *Ten-thirty*. Groaning, she rolled over and covered her head with a pillow to block out the bright morning sunshine. She had made it through another night without Cameron, and it was hell.

She hadn't seen or heard from him in days, but it was her own damn fault, wasn't it? She'd thrown his marriage proposal in his face, so what had she expected?

Maybe a phone call? An email? Maybe a demand to know her reasons? But no, she'd heard nothing.

Cameron hadn't even tried to change her mind when she'd said she couldn't marry him. He'd just snapped the velvet jeweler's box closed, apologized and drove her home. The silence had hung heavy in the dark car. It was one of the worse nights of her life.

Jessie swung her legs to the floor and stood. For a split second, she felt dizzy and caught hold of the bed poster for support. She waited for the room to stop spinning, before heading to the bathroom. She really needed to take better care of herself and stop wallowing in misery and self-pity. She'd only brought it on herself after all.

After washing her face and combing her hair, she felt somewhat better. In the kitchen, Jessie started the coffee maker and soon the lovely aroma of coffee filled the air. Pulling her robe closer around her shoulders, she stood at the kitchen sink and stared out the window, waiting for the coffee to brew.

Yeah, she should really stop indulging in this pity party. She'd gotten through some tough times in her life before this. She could do it again.

The coffee maker stopped gurgling and Jessie poured a cup of coffee. Hoping a jolt of caffeine would jump-start her body, she took a sip and the hot liquid scorched her tongue.

Good, she was beginning to feel again. Her whole body had been numb since Cameron had left her on her doorstep Friday evening. *Valentine's Day.* The day dedicated to love. The day she'd stomped on Cameron McCade's heart. The day he'd told her he loved her and wanted to marry her... and she'd refused.

What in the world was wrong with her? Her most secret wish had come true and she'd thrown it away? Why hadn't she talked to him about her not being able to have children? Why hadn't she told him she loved him?

Smooth, Jess. Just flat out refuse his love and proposal. She'd never been good with the man/woman thing. But that didn't begin to explain her actions. She must be sick in the head.

Jessie took another sip of coffee and squared her shoulders. She was through with crying. She'd go into work today and pretend nothing had happened. She should be thankful Cameron had returned to Salt Fork and was practicing at the clinic. That was one dream that had come true.

And if she had to live the rest of her life without the man she'd always loved? Jessie sighed. She seemed destined to live with some kind of regret hanging over her. She'd move on somehow. She always did.

* * *

Cameron rushed up the steps of City Hall, adjusting the tie he'd thrown on just minutes before. He'd almost forgotten the City Council meeting tonight. The meeting where he was going to be presented a plaque thanking him for taking the position at the clinic. Jessie would also be there, since she'd been the one to get the clinic up and running.

They'd planned on attending together, but that was *before*. Before Jessie had refused to be his wife.

And he hadn't had a chance to put any new plan into action. Hell, he'd been so busy he hadn't even thought of a plan. The flu had hit the residents of Salt Fork with a vengeance and Cameron was kept running from dawn to dusk, seeing patients.

When he opened the council chamber's doors, the first person he saw was Jessie. She was wearing that blue dress that had nearly driven him out of his mind with desire when she'd worn it to his mom's birthday party last fall. Damn, that seemed like a lifetime ago. So many things had changed since then.

Mayor Vandeford came forward to shake Cameron's hand, a welcoming smile on his face. "Dr. McCade, so glad you could make it."

Cameron shook hands with the man, eyes still focused on Jessie who was standing across the council chamber talking to a group of people. "I'm honored to be here. How's your daughter doing? She fully recovered from her accident at the homecoming game last fall?"

The mayor nodded. "Oh yes, and she's back to cheerleading which she loves. My Hilda's a little trooper. I can't thank you enough for your quick actions that night."

"No problem. That's my job. Glad to hear she's okay."

Just then the doors opened to admit more people, and Cameron was glad to see his mother, Austin, Kelsey and Tyler among the crowd. The mayor greeted the McCades, then turned away when someone asked him a question.

"Oh, Cam," Ruth said, a little out of breath. "I thought we were going to be late. I wouldn't miss this for the world. I'm so proud of you."

He hugged his mom and ruffled Kelsey's hair. "Dallas couldn't make it?"

Ruth sniffed and fished in the pocket of her coat for a tissue. "He's still angry about... well, you know."

Tyler smacked Cameron on the shoulder. "Don't worry about old Dallas. He can't stay mad forever."

Austin looked around the chambers. "Quite a crowd here tonight. We'd better grab some seats. Break a leg, Cam."

The mayor returned to Cameron's side. "Sorry about that. Duties and all. I'm sure you know most of the people here, but there are a few new faces. Let me introduce you around before the meeting gets underway."

As Cameron followed the mayor and shook hands with various councilmen, he kept Jessie in his peripheral line of vision. She'd glanced his way only once, then quickly looked away. She seemed pale. Was she ill or just uncomfortable?

Damn, he missed her. This situation was totally unnecessary. Two people who loved each other, enjoyed the same things and shared incredible sexual chemistry should be able to marry and have kids. What could possibly be keeping her from accepting his proposal?

The meeting was called to order. Cameron sat beside the mayor and Jessie sat three seats down the table.

Old business was discussed and Cameron listened with half an ear, his mind on his personal problems and what he could do to fix things between Jessie and himself.

Because if things weren't fixed soon, Cameron had the sick feeling that Jessie would be lost to him forever.

Jessie couldn't remember when she'd felt this uncomfortable and uneasy. With Cameron sitting so close, yet so far away, she was unable to keep her mind on the business at hand

In a few minutes, she was supposed to stand near Cameron and present him with a token of appreciation from the Chamber of Commerce. She was going to have to touch him while she fastened the gold pin to his jacket, smell his unique smell, feel the heat from his big body. The body she'd become intimately acquainted with over the past several months. The body belonging to the man she loved with all her heart, but had refused to marry.

What in the world was wrong with her?

"And now we come to the part of the program that's my favorite," the mayor announced. "Tonight, it's with great pleasure and honor that I present a hometown boy who has come back to roost, a man who has taken on a position that is near and dear to our hearts. Ladies and gentlemen, Dr. Cameron McCade."

Everyone stood and the room rocked with applause and whistles. Jessie watched from her vantage point as Cameron walked to the front of the council table where the mayor handed him a large wooden plaque.

Ruth and his brothers were sitting in the audience and Jessie could see the pride in Ruth's eyes as everyone applauded loud and long. Jessie craned her neck looking for Dallas, but he was nowhere to be seen. The big rancher was obviously still angry with Cameron. Maybe when he found out she'd refused to marry his brother, Dallas would forgive Cameron and be friends again. She should feel good about that, but it afforded her little comfort.

Mayor Vandeford looked Jessie's way and nodded. It was her turn. She swallowed her discomfort, took a deep breath and made her way to the podium. She was a grown woman. She could handle this. It would soon be over and she could go home to her empty house and have herself another good cry. Sooner or later, she'd run out of tears.

Jessie stood behind the podium and waited for the applause to die down before speaking. She kept her eyes forward, not wanting to look at Cameron before it was absolutely necessary. "I would also like to welcome Dr.

McCade back to Salt Fork," she said. "As president of the Chamber of Commerce, I'm happy to offer my heartfelt gratitude to him for filling a much-needed void in our community. Now, the citizens of Salt Fork can receive quick efficient medical treatment without having to drive eighty miles to the nearest hospital."

Jessie paused and took another deep breath. With her knees shaking and hands trembling, she hoped she could perform her part in this presentation without losing her composure and embarrassing herself.

Mayor Vandeford stepped back and Jessie walked over to stand beside Cameron. His blue eyes fastened on hers and she couldn't seem to break the contact.

She cleared her throat and stuck out her hand. Cameron took it in his warm grasp and the current of electricity flowing up her arm nearly short-circuited her brain cells. Time stood still in that moment. Then Cameron released her hand and Jessie tried to smile. She knew it must be a poor excuse for a smile, because she could feel her mouth trembling in time to her pounding heart.

Courage, Jessie. You can do this.

She cleared her throat again. "I'm honored to present you the Chamber of Commerce's 'Welcome to Town' golden pin." She opened the small plastic box and removed the pin. Taking hold of the lapel of Cameron's sport coat, the same one he'd worn to the Valentine's Dance, Jessie affixed the small golden pin, then quickly stepped away. The audience once again broke out in applause.

Cameron moved close and kissed her cheek. "Thank

you, Jess. This means a lot to me."

His deep beloved voice seeped into her very soul. Jessie couldn't speak, only nodded, her throat clogged with unshed tears. She needed to get out of here now. But she couldn't without being impossibly rude.

"Won't you say a few words, Dr. McCade?" Mayor Vandeford asked.

"Of course." Cameron winked at Jessie before taking his place at the podium. She couldn't stop the flutter in her heart. He'd given her a look like he wasn't through with her and her body thrummed with excitement and dread. He didn't look like a man whose marriage proposal had so recently been rejected.

Jessie didn't wait to hear what Cameron said to the crowd. She didn't care if she was acting rudely. She had to get home. She had to get away from Cameron McCade and the knowledge that she'd stupidly thrown away her last chance at happiness.

Cameron waited as long as he could before following Jessie to her house. The drive out of town took twenty minutes. Twenty minutes to figure out what he wanted to say.

He pulled off the pavement and headed down the winding dirt road leading to the Devine place. He hadn't been to her house since the Valentine's Dance. It seemed forever. He'd been too shocked the night she'd refused his proposal to ask her for her reasons. He'd gotten over the shock and was ready to hear those reasons now.

He was looking for answers, damn it. And tonight he'd get her to talk. And he'd get her into bed, too. His body ached to hold her again. Be inside her again. Make them one.

He parked the Jag in front of the house and walked up to the porch. The lights were on. Welcoming? Or warning him to stay away?

Too damned bad. He was here and there was no turning back.

Cameron knocked on the door and waited. His hands felt clammy and his heartbeat quickened.

After what seemed like an eternity, Jessie finally opened the door, then just stood there looking out the screen at him. The dog and cat flanked her, guarding her.

Hell, he wasn't the enemy. He loved her.

"Ask me in, Jess."

She bit her lip. "Why?"

Cameron took a deep breath. Now wasn't the time to lose his temper. "We need to talk."

Jessie nodded and opened the door. Cameron entered the living room. Sherlock barked once, then nudged his hand, inviting him to pet him.

Cameron rubbed the dog's ears, watching Jessie. She walked over to the heater and warmed her backside. She was still wearing the powder blue dress she'd worn to the council meeting.

God, he loved that dress. She'd worn it to his mother's party where he'd taken her to the barn and...

Cameron sighed. That was over four months ago. When they'd been fighting the attraction between them. When Jess had been fighting and he'd just wanted to get her into bed.

She was still fighting. But now, Cameron wanted more than just getting Jessie into bed. He wanted it all.

He closed the distance between them and took her in his arms. She belonged in his arms. Couldn't she feel it? Couldn't she feel the rightness? "I think it's time you told me why you think you can't marry me."

"You make it sound like I don't know my own mind," she said, trying to push away. He tightened his hold and she sighed. "I don't *think* I can't marry you, Cameron. I know I can't... shouldn't... let me go." Again, she tried to wiggle out of his arms.

"I don't want to let you go. Ever." Cameron stared deeply into Jess' eyes. Beautiful green eyes sparkling with tears. Something was definitely wrong.

He kissed the wet cheeks. He hated to see her so unhappy. "What's the matter, Jess? I thought you'd be happy that I was back in town. You told me it was your dream for me to take over the clinic. I thought you wanted me to move to Salt Fork. I thought you wanted me. Was I wrong?"

Jessie shook her head, her short blond hair bouncing with the movement. "I did want you... *do* want you–" She sniffed and swiped at her nose. "Damn. I'm not going to cry. I should just tell you what's bothering me, but I don't know how."

Cameron hugged her close and kissed the top of her forehead. "Try, Jess. I asked you to marry me, for crying out loud. I love you. And you love me; I *know* it. We can work this out, whatever it is. It can't be so very bad, can it?"

"It's pretty bad," she whispered, not looking at him, but fiddling with the gold pin on his jacket lapel. The pin she had presented to him only a couple of hours ago. "*I* think it's bad."

"Tell me, sweetheart."

He felt her stiffen in his arms, as if she were preparing herself for an assault or something.

"I can't have children," she blurted out. "You said you want kids. TR wanted a baby more than anything and I failed him. I promised myself not to do anything that I'd live to regret any more if I can help it. And I mean to stick to that promise."

"Look at me, Jess."

She shook her head and sniffled again.

Cameron's chest tightened. Jessie was one stubborn woman. If she decided something, it took an act of Congress to make her change her mind. He suddenly felt her slipping from him. He couldn't let her go, couldn't let her get away. He'd let her go once before. He couldn't do it again.

Tucking a finger beneath her chin, he tilted her head until she was forced to meet his gaze. "I love you, Jess. It's taken me a hell of a long time to realize that. I've lived with the restlessness my whole life. But when I came back for Mom's birthday party, the restless feeling left. And you know why? Because I found you again."

"But I can't marry you," she said with a sob. "I can't live with the knowledge I won't be able to give you children. I just can't do that again." A big tear slid down her cheek and Cameron caught it with his thumb. She was killing him. But she was hurting, too. He wanted to make her better. He was a doctor. It's what he did. Made people better.

"Did you have fertility tests done when you were married to TR?" he asked, stroking her soft hair.

Her head jerked up and she sniffed. "What?"

"Fertility tests. You know, to see if you were ovulating? Did TR have any tests done? How do you know it was your fault?"

Jessie shook her head and wiped her eyes. "He didn't want any tests done. He didn't want to get caught up in all of that technical stuff. Besides, those tests are expensive and the little insurance we had wouldn't cover them. TR just wanted it to happen naturally. He said if it happened, it happened. He was just being nice. I knew how disappointed he was. I can't do that to you, Cameron."

"Look, Jess. Forget about the kids," he said. "All I want is you. We could always adopt, you know."

"It wouldn't be the same." She wiggled out of his embrace and stepped away, crossing her arms, rubbing herself as if she were cold. "Maybe you'd better leave."

"I don't want to leave. In fact, I'm not leaving," he said, shucking off his jacket and throwing it on the couch. "I want you too much. Please, Jess. Make love with me."

"I don't think we should–"

He loosened his tie. "One more time, sweetheart. Let's make love one more time."

If only he could get her in bed, he believed he could change her mind. He wanted to make sweet love to her, seduce her, remind her what they had together. Remind her how many years they'd wasted already. They didn't need to waste another minute, as far as Cameron was concerned.

He took her in his arms again and captured her lips, tasting coffee and Jessie's own sweetness. She held back a few moments, and he thought he'd lost, thought she was going to refuse him, but finally she melted against him and he breathed a sigh of relief.

Cameron pulled her onto his lap and moved his body against her, prodding her warm softness, while plundering her sweet mouth. She moaned and wrapped her arms around his neck.

"We shouldn't do this," she said, her words vibrating against his lips.

"Shh, we're doing this."

Jessie sighed and he took the kiss deeper, plunging his tongue into her mouth, holding her close. She played with the hair at the nape of his neck. He loved when she did that. Suddenly, he was on fire and needed more than a kiss.

Jessie knew the instant the kiss changed from exploratory to hot and vital. Cameron cradled her butt in his big strong hands and lifted her against him, so she could feel his arousal and how much he wanted her.

"I need you, Jess," he growled in her ear, sending goose bumps flittering down her spine.

She couldn't fight the inevitable and gave herself up to the wonderful feelings of passion only this man could stoke deep within her. *One last time,* she thought. *One last time to be with Cameron.*

Jessie took his hand and brought it to her mouth. She

kissed the center of his palm. "Let's continue this in bed."

"Excellent idea." He smiled the sexy smile that always made her stomach crater. "Lead the way." With his hands on her shoulders, he followed her to the bedroom.

She pulled back the quilts on the large four-poster bed. The sound of Cameron's zipper shattered the quiet of the room and froze her in place. Jessie knew she really shouldn't be making love with Cameron again. Not when she'd already refused to marry him. But she could no more resist the desire burning between them than the urge to replace a noisy muffler on an old car. Her breath caught in her lungs when Cameron stood close behind, his naked body rubbing the thin cloth of her panties, his strong hands grasping her narrow waist, pulling her to him.

Cameron reached around to cup her breasts. "Watch my hands, Jess," he whispered in her ear, as he unfastened her bra.

Slowly the lacy material eased away from her rounded curves and the fabric teased her nipples. Cameron raked his nails softly across the satiny mounds, following the path of the lace with his fingers. He weighed her breasts in his palms, gently squeezing the firm flesh and brushing his thumbs across the nipples.

Jessie saw the rigid peaks pucker in response. Cameron's fingers traced the rosy ring at the center of each breast, outlining the curvature of the swells, dipping into the valley between, moving slowly up to the base, stopping just short of the nipples. He trailed light, feathery touches–some fast, some slow–over her sensitive skin. He focused his attention on the soft fleshy mounds, deliberately neglecting the tight swollen beads that ached to be touched.

He placed a finger to her lips. "Open your mouth."

Moistening his index finger against her tongue, he swirled the wetness around and around the base of her nipples, leaning over her shoulder to blow each one in turn.

Every nerve ending in Jessie's body tensed from the seductive torture. "Please..." she begged, her voice a ragged sob.

Cameron's fingers hovered above the nipples.

Jessie moaned low, as if in pain. She arched toward the teasing hands. "Cameron..."

He flicked the tips of the turgid peaks, lightly brushing across the sensitive beads. Once, twice. He kept his fingers close, barely making contact.

Jessie's body involuntarily bucked. She grabbed his hands and placed them on her breasts, urging him to caress her fully.

Cameron massaged the heated flesh. The sight of Jessie's white hands on top of his dark ones, helping him give her pleasure, threatened his control. He wedged one knee between her legs and rubbed back and forth. He felt her dampness on the top of his thigh. His erection throbbed and hardened even more. Lifting Jessie off the floor, he eased her onto the bed, flat on her stomach.

He tore her panties down the length of her legs and tossed them aside. Kneeling above her, Cameron kissed the curve of her neck. Her skin was soft and smooth. He trailed his tongue down her spine, kneaded both cheeks of her bottom with his hands, and licked the two dimples at the small of her back.

Suddenly, he flipped her over.

Jessie's eyes widened and dilated. She reached toward him. "Let me touch you," she whispered.

Cameron straddled her. He gritted his teeth as her fingers closed around him, caressing, stroking.

He moved away. "Keep that up, and we'll be finished before we're good and started."

Her husky laugh titillated his senses. He took her mouth in a hot savage kiss. She held him close and matched the movements of his tongue with her own.

Cameron stretched out beside her. He kissed her again, dipping into the honeyed flavor only Jessie could provide. He butted his shaft against her thigh and felt the urgent need to plunge himself into her. But not yet. Not yet.

He kissed the corners of her mouth and the tip of her nose, then pulled away. Jessie groaned in disappointment and sought to bring him close again. Gently, he pushed her back against the pillows. "I want to kiss you all over, sweetheart."

He took one nipple into his mouth and sucked hard. A deep moan erupted from Jessie's throat. Sliding his hand down her flat stomach, he twined his fingers in her soft curls. Gently, he teased the velvety folds, lightly brushing, touching, applying the same sweet torture he'd inflicted on her breasts just minutes before.

Jessie gripped his shoulders. Her nails bit deeply into his skin. Cameron bent to lave her navel with his tongue, then trailed kisses down her abdomen. He stopped just above the dark triangle of hair and looked up. Jessie's face was flushed with desire, her eyes drugged with passion.

Cameron felt himself flex in response to the yearning in those eyes. Slowly, ever so slowly, he spread open the soft folds with gentle fingers. Softly, so softly, he nuzzled her most intimate flesh.

Jessie's hips bucked upward. The exquisite rasp of Cameron's tongue released the surge of tension he had so expertly nurtured. She tangled her fingers in his hair, trying to find a handhold, as her body erupted in pleasure.

"Now, Cameron," she said. "I need you."

He pulled her beneath him and spread her legs apart. Lowering himself, he slid inside her moist heat. He waited a moment, enjoying the feel of Jessie's warm flesh holding him, caressing him.

"Please, Cameron." Jessie cupped his jaws with trembling fingers.

He turned his head to kiss each palm, then started making love to her. He moved over her, in her. Deep inside, then away. Pull and push. Slow, then fast. Jessie matched his thrusts, her inner muscles contracting, squeezing him.

Cameron groaned with satisfaction as his body convulsed in orgasm. Jessie rubbed his back and kissed his neck. His last conscious thought was that a man couldn't ask for much more than this and somehow, some way he had to make Jessie change her mind about marrying him.

* * *

"Nothing has changed," Jessie said, lying in the darkness of her room, with Cameron beside her in bed. "I'm still not marrying you."

Cameron slammed his fist on top of the sheets. "For crying out loud, Jess. How can you say that after what we just shared?"

Jessie shot up out of bed, grabbed a robe and hauled it on, all the while conscious of Cameron's frowning eyes upon her. She smoothed back her hair and turned to face the angry man in her bed. Naked. Still. Unconcerned with his lack of clothes. Looking incredibly sexy amidst the rumpled sheets.

"I told you I can't have babies. I can't live knowing I'm denying you something you want."

Cameron rose out of bed and stood before her, hands on hips. "You are denying me something I want. Very badly. More than I want kids."

"What are you talking about?"

"I want you, Jess. I want to marry you, share my life with you. I want to make love to you every night and wake up each morning with you by my side. How can you live with knowing how much I want you and not having you? You're denying both of us something we want desperately."

Jessie shook her head. "I just can't. You don't understand."

"No, I don't understand." Cameron dragged on his boxers, then his slacks. "Before you throw both our futures away, why don't you have a fertility test just to make sure? We've been having unprotected sex for months, and you might be carrying my child even now."

"I'm not," she said. "I can't be. I'm barren, I tell you. We've been intimate since last October, and I haven't missed a period in all that time. Sure, they've been irregular, but they've always been that way. And that's probably too much information, but you asked. Face it, Cameron. I faced it a long time ago. I'll never be able to have children. I'm sorry."

Cameron strode toward her and glared down at her. "You are one stubborn woman. You know that?"

"I think you should leave."

He pulled on his shirt and hastily buttoned it up. "Oh, I'm leaving all right. But this isn't over, sweetheart. Not by a long shot."

He swiped his tie from the floor and flung it around his neck, his blue eyes spitting fire. "Don't bother showing me the door. I know the way. Good bye, Jess."

CHAPTER TWELVE

*T*he days following the council meeting proved to be extremely difficult. Jessie forced herself to go to work, but she didn't get much done. She was horrified that she'd made love with Cameron knowing she wasn't going to marry him or have any kind of relationship with him. She knew she was weak where he was concerned, but she should have stood firm and sent him on his way instead of falling into bed with him.

Her heart felt heavy and she was depressed. On top of all that, her tummy started acting up at the end of the week and she hoped she wasn't coming down with the flu that was going around town. At noon on Friday, Sam sent her home.

"You need to go to bed, Jessie. You look awful."

"Gee, thanks. Just what a girl wants to hear."

Sam wiped his hands on a grease rag. "I don't think you want to hear what I really have a mind to say. You need to take better care of yourself. Go home, Jess. I'll take care of things here."

"Thanks, Sam. I think I might have caught a bug. I'll take the weekend off and see you on Monday."

"Sure thing, Boss Lady." Sam smiled and held the door for her.

Jessie got her purse and her coat. "If you need anything, just call. I'm not bedridden yet."

"You will be if you don't get some rest. Now, *git*."

"Yes, sir."

Before heading home, Jessie stopped at the café for a bowl of soup. It was lunch hour and thankfully, Sarah Sue was too busy to pry. Jessie didn't feel like fielding questions about her love life. Her nonexistent love life as of a couple of weeks ago. Not counting that moment of weakness after the council meeting.

The soup soothed her stomach, but not the turmoil in her soul. Damn, she'd never thought making the decision not to marry Cameron would hurt so much.

Hadn't she decided it was better to continue living without him, than to marry him and not be able to give him children? And hadn't she reasoned to herself that it was all for the best so she wouldn't be a constant thorn in Dallas' side causing a rift between the two brothers?

Yeah, right, Jess. Who do you think you're fooling? It looked like a lose/lose proposition no matter which path she chose. If she married Cameron, she'd feel horrible because she couldn't bear his children. On the other hand, if she didn't marry him, she would still live in misery spurning the man she'd always loved.

Something he'd thrown in her face, by the way.

More than just spurning him, but keeping him from something he wanted much more than children. He wanted *her*.

Either way, either choice she made, she would end up disappointing him.

Bumping along the dirt road in her old pickup truck, these thoughts circled inside Jessie's head. When she rounded the stand of mesquite trees guarding the house, she stomped on the brakes and screeched to a halt. *What in the world?*

The front porch looked like Gussie Ferguson's Florist Shop. Vases of all shapes and sizes covered every inch of her porch each overflowing with dark red roses.

Katnip and Sherlock emerged from the midst of the bower and came forward to greet Jessie.

She climbed out of the truck and slammed the door behind her. As if in a dream, she walked up the stone path, stopped at the porch step and just stared at the bounty of roses nestled together making the old porch a beautiful sight to behold.

Tears formed in her eyes and she swallowed a lump in her throat. She stepped up onto the porch and sat down amongst the flowers. She counted seventeen arrangements of the most gorgeous long-stemmed roses she'd ever seen. Or maybe they were gorgeous because she'd never received many flowers in her life. Or maybe it was because they were from the man she loved.

She knew they were from Cameron. Who else? Searching every bouquet and spray of roses, Jessie finally found a card and plucked it from the vase closest to where she sat. With trembling fingers she opened the small envelope and read the bold handwriting.

To Jess, the woman who holds my heart. Please accept these small tokens of my affection, one for every year we've wasted not being together. My love stands true. My heart belongs to you. Know you are in my thoughts every second of every day. I love you, Cameron.

Jessie held the card to her heart and closed her eyes. The sweet subtle fragrance of the roses wafted around her, lulling her, whispering to her, battling the defenses she'd worked so hard to erect around her heart.

She stood, weak-kneed and a little wobbly, and slowly entered the house. She read the love note again, knowing a chink of her self-imposed armor had been chiseled loose.

Be strong, Jess. Be strong.

Monday morning, Jessie was late for work. She'd spent the weekend tossing and turning, getting little rest and less sleep. When she did manage to sleep, she dreamed of the roses and Cameron McCade. His smile, his eyes, his lovemaking. How he'd given up his life in Houston and returned to Salt Fork. How he'd said he loved her and wanted to spend his life with her.

When she wasn't sleeping, Jessie lay in bed staring at the ceiling thinking about what she'd let slip through her fingers. What could have been such a happy life with Cameron.

If only...

She'd moved the roses inside the house. Every time she walked to the kitchen to make soup or tea, seventeen vases of lovely roses reminded her of what she'd given up.

Pulling up behind the garage, Jessie parked her truck and immediately made her way to the office. Sam hollered a greeting from under the sedan he was working on. Since she wasn't in the mood to be around people, she hoped Sam would work in the garage most of the day. She had a ton of paper work to plow through.

When Jessie jerked opened the door to the office, her hand froze on the metal handle. A rainbow of color bombarded her–on top of the desk, the file cabinet and even on the ancient swivel chair. Baskets and baskets full of carnations. Seventeen. She knew without counting.

The bell on the door jingled and Sam came in. "Seems like you've got an admirer. McCade sure seems determined. I bet he's going to ask you to marry him. Congratulations, Jessie."

Jessie's stomach rolled over and she suddenly felt sick. Sicker than she'd felt all weekend. And dizzy. So dizzy, she sank down into the straight-backed chair in front of the desk before she could faint right then and there.

Sam rushed over and stood in front of her, a frown creasing his black brows. "Are you sure you should have come in to work? Maybe you're not over that stomach virus. You should have stayed home another day. Maybe you should go to the clinic and see the doctor–"

"No!" Jessie shook her head. Good lord, she didn't

want to see Cameron. It would hurt too much. "I'm fine. I'm still recovering, but I'm well enough to work. I'll take it easy and stay in here, catch up on the accounts receivable and let you take care of the repairs." She took a deep breath and conjured up a smile. "Could you help move the flowers to the floor, so I can get to the computer?"

"Sure thing. You just sit there and rest. Want some water or something?"

"Water would be nice."

Jessie sipped her bottle of cold water while Sam cleared the desk and chair.

"There's a card in this basket," he said and handed it to her. "Yeah, McCade is one determined man. I'll get back to the transmission I'm working on. If you need anything, just holler."

Jessie gingerly rose from the chair and rounded the desk, sinking into the swivel chair. For a minute, she sat there staring at the card in her hand, afraid to open it.

With a huge breath, she berated herself for being a coward and quickly slit open the envelope.

These flowers can't begin to express the love I feel for you. I need you like I need air to breathe and sunshine to live. Seventeen years ago, I made a wrong turn. Help me find the way back, Jess. I love you, Cameron.

Jessie stared at the card. Seventeen years ago, Cameron had asked her to the prom and her life miraculously changed. She remembered how surprised and shocked she'd been when he'd shown up at the garage one week before the big event. She couldn't believe he'd asked her to be his date.

Jessie looked at the baskets of carnations surrounding her on the floor of the office. Yes, she'd lost her heart to Cameron McCade seventeen years ago. And when he'd kissed her up on Lover's Point that night, her world had tilted and it had never been the same since.

He'd been like Prince Charming, awakening her to love and desire. Then he'd left her high and dry.

Cameron had called her stubborn, but if she hadn't had that stubborn streak, Jessie would never have survived when he went off to college and left her. She'd never have survived the ordeal of taking care of her sick father. Or losing her mother at such a tender age. Or watching TR die, knowing she hadn't loved him as she should have.

Jessie knew she was capable of living without Cameron, but she wanted to cry when she thought of the bleak empty future stretching before her.

It wouldn't be easy. Lord, it had never been easy. And it was different now. Cameron wasn't far away anymore.

No, the man she loved was back in Salt Fork. And he loved her and wanted to marry her. She would see him around town, run into him, constantly be aware of his presence over at the clinic or in his house in the middle of town.

Jessie looked at the flowers surrounding her. He obviously wasn't going to make it easy for her either. He seemed to be laying siege to her heart, deliberately battling down her defenses.

She sighed. Hadn't she always wished she could be

part of his plans? That wish had finally come true.

Jessie felt her resolve slipping. She brushed her fingers over the petals of a yellow carnation. The flowers lit up the office like Cameron lit up her life. He'd told her he wanted her more than he wanted kids. Could she believe him?

How would she survive, living in the same town as Cameron, knowing she'd disappointed him by not marrying him? How could she marry him, unable to give him a child?

She'd been over the argument again and again. No wonder she was dizzy.

Jessie booted up the computer. Thank God, she now had the resources and money to pay most of the bills. She couldn't have lived with herself if she'd screwed up and lost the garage on top of everything else.

And that was another thing.

Dallas McCade was angry about her leasing the oil rights on his ranch. As far as she knew, he still wasn't talking to Cameron. He certainly wasn't talking to her. Which wasn't such a bad thing, considering he only hounded her about selling the mineral rights when he did speak to her.

Always a silver lining somewhere in there, right?

That's stretching it a bit, Jess.

She pulled up the accounts receivable and set to work. She'd lose herself in the dreary columns of numbers for now and let the future take care of itself.

* * *

At five o'clock, Cameron hung his lab coat on the hook behind his office door, grabbed his Stetson and the gaily-wrapped gift from his desk and headed out the clinic door. Sheila would lock up as she always did.

They'd settled into a nice routine–he opened the clinic in the morning; she closed at night. It worked out great for both of them. Cameron whistled a happy tune as he drove down the road toward the café.

He wondered how Jessie had reacted to all the flowers he'd sent. And the notes he'd written, agonizing over every word. He'd realized Jessie had never really dated, had never been courted or wooed, to use the old-fashioned terms.

She'd always been more of a tomboy, working in the garage with her father. She'd never worn frilly, girlie outfits when she'd been a kid. She still preferred jeans, but once in a while when she wore something like that powder-blue dress that drove him crazy, there was no doubt that she was one sexy woman.

He turned into the café parking lot, eased the car into a slot and cut the engine. Jessie wasn't beautiful in the classical sense. She was more cute than pretty. But she was beautiful to Cameron. It didn't matter what she had on. And naturally, he liked her best with nothing on at all.

He gripped the steering wheel. If she didn't respond to his overtures of wooing, he didn't know what he would do. He couldn't imagine continuing to live in Salt Fork without Jessie by his side.

As usual, the café was crowded at this time of day. Cameron found a seat at the counter, laid the package in front of him and waited for Sarah Sue to come by with his water and menu.

"Well, hey there, sugar!" Sarah Sue said, hurrying over. "Haven't seen you in quite a while. Been busy getting settled at the clinic? How's the new house coming along? I've always admired the old Peterson house. You are one lucky man that it came on the market when it did and Jessie was able to put down your money for you. By the way, when are you and Jessie going to make up? She's moping around like I don't know what. And when are you going to stop dragging your feet and ask that girl to marry you?"

Cameron smoothed the ribbon on the package. He hated to admit anything to anybody, but maybe Sarah Sue could help him out. She and Jessie were close friends. But from the sound of it, Jessie hadn't told Sarah Sue the recent developments in their relationship. A relationship he felt slipping from him with every passing minute.

"I guess you haven't talked to Jessie lately," he said. "She hasn't told you–"

"Hey, Sarah Sue! Can I get some service over here?" someone called from the corner.

"Hold your horses, Shorty. I'm coming." Sarah Sue bent to retrieve menus from behind the counter. "Don't you move, Cameron McCade. I want to know what's going on. Jessie's been feeling mighty poorly lately and she's been closed as an oyster about everything. Figure out what you want to eat, while I take care of a few customers."

She shoved a menu in Cameron's hands and whisked

away. Five minutes ago, he'd been hungry as a bear. Now, he couldn't think about eating.

Before he even opened the menu, Sarah Sue was back, standing beside him instead of behind the counter. She whipped the menu from his grasp. "Let's go, darlin'."

"Where to?"

"My office." She grabbed his hand and pulled him out of his seat. He barely had time to pick up the wrapped package from the counter. "We need to discuss this in private," she said, dragging him along. "I may like to gossip, but not about Jessie's private life."

Cameron followed her through the swinging doors leading to the kitchen, past the stoves and super-sized refrigerator, into a tiny room in the corner of the building.

She closed the door and pointed to a chair. "Sit."

Cameron had to smile. Sarah Sue wasn't actually old enough to be his mother, but she sure sounded like a mom. "Yes'm," he said, sliding into the straight-backed chair facing the old metal desk.

Sarah Sue hitched a hip on the desk, crossed her arms over her meager bosom and glared at him. "Okay, I'm all ears. Tell me everything. I should have known Jessie would screw things up. If ever I saw such a stubborn person... well, I haven't, and that's the truth. So spill it, sugar."

Cameron set the package on the desktop and Sarah Sue eyed it with a gleam in her eyes. He took off his Stetson and settled more comfortably in the hard chair, not knowing how much to tell. He wasn't used to revealing things about himself to anyone.

"Honey, I'm on your side and Jessie's, of course. I take it from what you almost told me out there that you've already asked her to marry you?"

"Yes, on Valentine's Day."

"And she refused you?"

He nodded.

Sarah Sue let out a huge exasperated sigh. "That girl. What in the world is going on in her stubborn little head? She's been in love with you since prom night. Did you know that?"

Cameron shook his head. "I knew she had a crush on me, but–"

"It was more than a crush," said Sarah Sue. "She was devastated when you left for college."

"We barely knew one another. How can that be?"

"Her crush and admiration turned into love, sugar. You were a mighty handsome boy. Nice, polite and charming, as well. A deadly combination for a young girl. Especially one with little experience, if you know what I mean?"

Cameron felt like squirming in the chair. This was turning out to be an uncomfortable conversation.

"What reason did she give you for turning down your marriage proposal?" Sarah Sue asked.

"Some malarkey about not being able to have children," he said. "I told her we could adopt. I even offered to pay for fertility testing. How does she know the fault was hers when she couldn't get pregnant with TR?"

"She couldn't. She just assumed." Sarah Sue looked

up at the ceiling and shook her head. "I thought I'd talked her out of those thoughts. Jessie has always been a glum little thing. Probably comes from losing her mama at such an early age. I did what I could for her, but no one can replace a girl's mother."

"You've been a good friend to her," Cameron said. "She's lucky to have you."

"Well, thank you, sugar. That's mighty nice of you. Now, what are you going to do about the situation?"

Cameron told her about the flowers and the notes he'd written. "I'm trying to think of romantic things to do to show Jessie I'm not taking no for an answer."

Sarah Sue smiled. "All those flowers delivered and I haven't heard a thing about it. Gussie Ferguson hasn't breathed a word to a soul."

"I asked her not to," Cameron said. "Garza promised not to spread it about either."

"So, what's your next move?" Sarah Sue asked, eying the wrapped package sitting on her desk.

Cameron picked it up and handed it to her. "I know Jessie comes in here several nights a week. I want you to give that to her, next time she stops by the café."

"What is it?"

Cameron stood and picked up his Stetson. "You'll have to wait until Jessie opens it." He kissed her cheek and left her gaping after him, feeling better than he had in days.

Jessie felt sicker than she had last week. In fact, she

was more nauseous than ever. She'd even thrown up yesterday morning. Sam had made her stay in the office for the past couple of days, saying he didn't like the way she looked. Badgering her to go see the doctor. Sam had asked her what good was there in having a clinic in town, if she didn't make full use of it.

Well, Sam hadn't slept with the resident physician or refused an offer of marriage from him. That made it just a tad embarrassing to make an appointment.

After the garage closed for the night, Jessie decided to visit Sarah Sue. Maybe have a bowl of soup and a few crackers; something to settle her riotous stomach. If she wasn't better soon, Jessie would be forced to see a doctor and she didn't feel like driving the eighty miles to Abilene. She'd have to swallow her embarrassment and make an appointment at the clinic.

Hopefully, she could see Cameron as a patient and they could keep things professional. Hopefully, when she saw him, she wouldn't burst into tears. Hopefully, she'd get well and wouldn't have to go see him.

The café was empty as usual when Jessie stopped by after work. Nine-thirty at night and most everyone had gone home, even the other waitress and the chef. Only Sarah Sue stayed late at the café, catching up on paper work, trying out new recipes. That was the only time she could cook in the kitchen without causing an uproar with her chef. He didn't like anyone trespassing on his domain, not even Sarah Sue.

Many a night, Jessie sat in the big kitchen and watched Sarah Sue make pies and pastries. They'd laugh and talk and gossip. Those times were some of Jessie's favorites.

She entered the café and spotted her friend through the kitchen window. "Hey there, darlin'," Sarah Sue said with a wave and a smile. "You're just in time. I have a peach cobbler in the oven. We'll have warm cobbler and ice cream in a few minutes. Come on back here."

Jessie swallowed and shook her head. "I'll take a rain check on that. All I want is some soup, if you have any."

Sarah Sue wiped her flour-dusted hands on her apron and pulled Jessie to the table sitting near the fridge. "You still feeling puny? You sit right here and I'll get you a bowl of potato soup. It'll soothe your stomach, I guarantee."

"Thanks. I'd like that."

Sarah Sue bustled around the large kitchen, opening the door of the stainless steel refrigerator, ladling a bowlful of soup and zapping it in the microwave. In no time flat, she set the steaming bowl in front of Jessie, with a sleeve of crackers and a tall glass of tea.

"Eat up. Then I have a surprise for you."

Jessie dipped her spoon in the soup and sipped it, making sure it wasn't too hot. The creamy liquid slid down her throat and settled in her agitated stomach, instantly making her feel better. "This is good. Just what I need."

Sarah Sue sat down across from her. "I could tell you what you need, but since you're so sick, I'll wait until you're better."

"It's okay. What do you think I need?"

"A swift kick in the rear, that's what."

Jessie's head jerked up and she stared at her friend. "Why would you say something like that?"

Sarah Sue sat back in her chair and crossed her arms over her chest. "Cameron McCade came in here today. He told me he asked you to marry him and you refused. I think you're sick in the head, darlin'."

Jessie laid her spoon aside. "I believe you're right."

"What were you thinking? You love that man to distraction, and he loves you. I can't believe you're giving up a lifetime of happiness and love just because you think you can't give that man babies."

Rubbing her temples, Jessie sighed. "I'm so confused I think that's what's making me feel so sick. I don't want to disappoint Cameron by not giving him children, but like he said, I'm still disappointing him by not marrying him, because he wants me, needs me. And I need him, too." God, how she needed him.

"Of course you need him," Sarah Sue said. "Didn't you tell me you were finished doing things you'd regret or feel guilty about?"

"Yes, but–"

Sarah Sue lifted a hand as if to ward off any argument. "Hear me out, Jessie. Do you regret making love with Cameron? You were confused about that, too. Remember? Are you sorry you slept with the man?"

"No, I'm not, but–"

"Do you love him?"

"Yes, but–"

"No buts. You love him. He loves you. Are you sorry you refused him? Do you regret that you won't be marrying him and living a full rich life with him?

Adopting children and raising them, if need be? Don't you regret that?"

"Yes! Okay, okay. Maybe I made a mistake."

Sarah Sue reached across the table and patted Jessie's hand. "There's no maybe about it. It's not too late, darlin'. He wants you more than ever."

"And I want him. But I'm scared." Scared spitless, in fact.

Sarah Sue patted her hand again. "Scared he'll leave? Scared you'll lose him? Like you lost your mama and daddy and TR?"

"Yes," Jessie whispered, realization suddenly dawning. "I'm scared to make the commitment. Scared to lay my heart open again."

Squeezing her hand, Sarah Sue gave it a little shake. "You have to take risks, darlin'. Cameron's not going to leave you again. Hell, he uprooted his life to be near you. He's made the commitment. Why can't you? Wait right here. He left something in my office that he wanted me to give you."

Jessie couldn't imagine what Cameron had done now. After the two deliveries of flowers, she didn't know what to expect.

Sarah Sue came back into the kitchen carrying a small thin square package. "Here you go. Open it. I'm dying to know what's in it."

Jessie held the package for a moment. Just like she'd been hesitant to open the envelopes that arrived with the flowers, she was hesitant to open the package.

"Well, go ahead. Open it, why don't you?" Sarah Sue said.

Jessie tore the paper and unwrapped a gold metal frame containing an old photograph. One taken seventeen years ago with a younger version of Jessie dressed in an ivory-colored prom dress looking dreamily up at her handsome escort wearing a black tuxedo and a baby-blue shirt. The photographer had caught the adoration and happiness Jessie remembered feeling that night.

She traced the image of the younger Cameron with a trembling finger. She'd forgotten about the picture taken that night. Somehow, she'd never seen it before. After Cameron had left her and moved away, she'd been too upset to think of photographs or much of anything else.

"Can I see?" Sarah Sue asked.

Jessie blinked away tears and handed the picture to her friend.

"Well, I'll be. That man has a romantic streak a mile wide. He told me about the flowers. *And now this*. You two made a mighty fine pair back then. Looks like you belong together, if you ask me. Is there a note in the wrappings?"

Jessie dashed a hand across her eyes, then searched through the brightly colored paper. "No, there's nothing."

Sarah Sue flipped the frame over. "Here's something."

Jessie took the frame and removed the tiny envelope taped to the back. There was something hard inside.

What in the world?

With shaking hands, Jessie opened the envelope and removed a small card and a key. Her heart pounded in her chest and she had trouble breathing. She sat there, turning the key over and over and over.

"Read the note, for crying out loud," Sarah Sue said.

The card was upside down. Jessie turned it so she could read the words, written in the now familiar bold handwriting.

You already hold the key to my heart and soul. You wouldn't accept my ring, but I hope you accept this gift. Here's the key to something I hold dear, but not nearly as dear as I hold you. Hope you enjoy the car. Love always, Cameron.

P.S. It's parked behind the café.

Jessie laughed and cried and held the key against her own rapidly thumping heart.

"What is it?" Sarah Sue demanded. "What is that key to?"

"His Jaguar. He gave me his Jag."

"Good God, he's as crazy as you are. Crazy about you, too. You need to quit this foolishness, darlin', and put that man out of his misery and tell him that you'll marry him."

"I can't accept the car. Can I?" *Could she?*

Sarah Sue nodded. "You can if you marry him. *Are* you going to marry him?"

Jessie looked at the note again, then at the key, then at the old photograph. Suddenly, she felt better than she had in months. "Yes, I am. I'm going to marry Cameron McCade!"

CHAPTER THIRTEEN

Cameron paced around the living room of his new home, wondering how Jessie would react to this latest surprise. He wondered if she'd even gone to Sarah Sue's tonight. She didn't stop at the café every night of the week, after all.

And he wondered what her reaction would be when she found the Jag parked behind the café. Would she be angry? Or would she finally believe he wanted her more than anything he'd ever wanted in his life? By giving her the Jag, he hoped she'd get it through her stubborn brain that he was serious about wanting to marry her and spend his life with her by his side.

The sound of a powerful engine pulling into his driveway made him smile. He hoped like hell she had changed her mind, because he was fast running out of ideas to convince her that he loved her and needed her.

He went to the door, opened it and waited for Jessie

to climb out of the car. He'd told her in the note that she held the key to his heart and soul, but she also held the key to his future happiness. Which would it be? A lifetime of love? Or the prospect of a bleak lonely existence?

Jessie ran up the walk and flung herself at Cameron, wrapping her arms around his neck, laughing and crying and kissing him like there was no tomorrow.

The heaviness in his heart lifted and he hugged her tightly, returning her kisses, loving the feel of her in his arms, inhaling her sweetness.

"Oh my God, Cameron! I can't believe you would give me your Jag. And all those flowers. And the notes." She sniffed and touched her fingers to his cheeks. "And the prom picture. I'd never seen it before, you know. Did Ruth have it stashed away somewhere? I'm surprised she didn't give me a copy years ago."

He clasped her fingers with his. "I never showed it to Mom," he said, kissing each finger in turn.

Her breath hitched at the intimate contact. "And you've kept it all these years?"

He pulled her closer and kissed her gently. "I took it with me when I left for college. I tucked it away in a book for safe keeping with all the moving I was doing. I hadn't seen it since grad school. I found it when I was unpacking some of my things a couple of weeks ago– Hey, where are you going?"

Jessie wiggled out of Cameron's arms and held out the keys to the Jaguar. He just stared at them, not making a move to take them. Was she refusing him again?

"You don't need to give me your car," she said. "I know how much it means to you."

"Not as much as you mean to me, Jess. I–"

She held up her hands to keep him at bay. "Please let me finish. The car is a lovely gesture, but the prom picture is the best gift of all, better than the flowers. If the offer's still good, I'd like to take you up on it."

"Of course, the offer's still good." He grabbed her waist and pulled her into his embrace again. "I love you so much, Jess." He touched her cheek and kissed her again, loving how well they fit together. Relieved that she'd finally agreed to be his wife.

Jessie's lungs constricted; something invisible squeezed her mid-section. She wanted Cameron with all her heart, but there were issues to discuss. She had to make perfectly certain. She tried to pull away, but his arms tightened around her, and he deepened the kiss.

After giving in for a heart-pounding moment, Jessie pushed at his chest and broke contact. "Please let me go, Cameron."

"I'm never letting you go again," he said, holding her close. "When I left Salt Fork, I had only one regret. Do you know what it was?"

She searched his face. "No, what?"

"Leaving you behind." He kissed her to ease the sting of the memory. "Even then, I knew there was something special and powerful between us. It scared the hell out of me. I couldn't stay. I had to get away. I had made my plans."

Jessie nodded. "I remember. I had a different future mapped out for myself, too. When Dad got sick, everything changed."

"I know, sweetheart. It must have been damned difficult. I'm sorry I wasn't there for you. I'm sorry I ever left you." Cameron smoothed the wisps of hair from her face. "I'm here now and we're together. We'll make up for lost time, I promise."

Jessie bit her lip. "What about your brother?"

Cameron hugged her. "What about him?"

"I leased the mineral rights on the ranch, remember? Dallas hates me and may never forgive me. And he isn't speaking to you. If we marry, he may never speak to you again."

"Dallas will get over it. We're too close and there's too much between us for him to stay angry forever. I want to marry you. Say you want to marry me, too."

Jessie's heart ricocheted in her chest as she hugged Cameron and kissed him again. Now, she was afraid because everything she'd ever wanted had suddenly come true. She was still afraid it might disappear just as quickly.

Cameron lifted her into his arms and carried her up the stairs. Jessie laughed again and looped her arms around his neck. "Hey, what do you think you're doing?"

"I need more than kisses. *We* need more than kisses. We need a bed."

Reaching his bedroom, he laid her on the mattress and followed her down. He started to kiss her, then pulled back and frowned.

"What's wrong?" Jessie asked, luxuriating in the feel of Cameron's weight bearing down on her.

"You haven't said yes," he said, his blue eyes gazing into hers.

Her tummy fluttered in response. "What do you mean?"

"I've asked you to marry me, and you haven't given me your answer." He brushed his hand across Jessie's soft hair. "I'm asking you again, Jess. Will you marry me?"

As long as she lived, she'd never get over thrill of being with this man. Smiling, Jessie kissed him. "Yes, Cameron. *Definitely yes!"*

A few hours later, Jessie lay snuggled against Cameron, her head on his shoulder, her leg thrown across his lower body. Happiness bubbled inside her.

A low chuckle deep in his chest vibrated against her ear. Raising herself on one elbow, she looked at him. "What's so funny? Why are you laughing?"

Cameron grinned. "I was just thinking how happy my mother is going to be."

Jessie lay back down. "You mean because you're finally putting your bachelor days behind you and getting married?"

"There's that, of course," he said with a nod. "But I was thinking more about the mineral rights."

Jessie raised up again. "What about the mineral rights?"

He chuckled. "When I came home that first time in October, Mom and Dallas told me about everything, how Copper River Oil was snooping around, and how *you* owned some of the mineral rights on the Diamondback Ranch–"

"Get to the point, Cameron."

"You know what my mother is," he said with amusement.

"Yes, she's a delightful fluff-head," Jessie answered fondly.

"Exactly. And you of all people know how much Dallas wants the mineral rights back in the family?"

"How could I ever forget?" She wrinkled her nose at the thought of all the confrontations with Dallas McCade in the past and maybe even a few in the not-so-distant future.

Cameron gave her a little squeeze. "Well get this: Mom had the bright idea that I should marry you, and then the whole mess would be solved. She'd have a daughter-in-law, the prospect of more grandkids, *and* as an added bonus, the mineral rights would be back in the family."

Cameron laughed again. "She'll be so happy and pleased with herself. It won't take long for her to believe she arranged this whole thing."

Jessie could just imagine Ruth feeling like that. Feeling glad about them marrying. But she wouldn't be glad about not getting any more grandchildren. Then another thought flashed unbidden in her mind.

Jessie pushed away and sat up. A sinking sensation burned in the pit of her stomach as that unwelcome thought expanded.

"Cameron?"

"What is it, sweetheart?" He slid his hands down her body, loving the feel of her beneath his fingers.

"If I marry you–" she began.

"If?" His hands stopped their exploration.

"Won't I be breaking my promise to TR? The mineral rights *will* be back in your family. I can't break my promise. I gave him my word." She sat back on her knees, her lips trembling.

Cameron wiped a tear from her cheek. "You are going to have to stop thinking of all these obstacles that could keep us from being together. Don't you *want* to marry me?"

"Of course I do. But a promise is a promise."

"Look, you promised TR you wouldn't *sell* the mineral rights to Dallas. You're not selling. We'll put the damn things in a trust for our kids. That will satisfy your promise *and* appease my brother."

"You're forgetting I can't get pregnant."

Cameron sighed. "If you're really unable to have children, then we'll adopt, like I told you before. There are many, many children in foster homes who need someone to love and take care of them. We could love and take care of a few, couldn't we, Jess? They'd be ours, no matter how they came into this world. I know you'll make a wonderful mother."

Cameron leaned over and opened the drawer in the bedside table. He pulled out the black velvet box and snapped it open, retrieving the diamond ring she'd refused on Valentine's Day. He took her left hand in his and looked deeply into her eyes. Jessie felt as if he were searching her very soul.

Silently, he slid the ring on the third finger of her left hand. The diamond glittered with a fire of its own, reminding Jessie of the fire burning in Cameron's eyes whenever he looked her way. Reminding her of the fire that burned between them, the fire that had always burned between them.

"With this ring," he said, his voice low and intense, "I want to make you my wife. I want you to be the mother of our children, no matter where they come from." He kissed the ring, then turned her hand over and kissed her palm. He twined his fingers with hers. "What do you say, Jess? Are you with me on this?"

Jessie nodded and felt tears gather in her eyes. For the first time, she really believed what Cameron had been trying to tell her all along. It didn't matter to him if she couldn't give him a child. He loved her and wanted to spend their lives together.

He squeezed her hand. "What do you say, sweetheart?"

Jessie smiled and launched herself against him. All was right with her world again. "I love you, Cameron McCade. I've loved you forever and ever."

Cameron held her in his arms, close to his heart. "It's about time you told me, Jess. It's about damned time you told me."

For the next couple of days, Jessie floated on a cloud of happiness. She'd practically moved in with Cameron already. They'd told Ruth they were getting married and as predicted, Cameron's mother was ecstatic over the news.

Jessie had come into work early today and was under Joe Montoya's truck changing the oil, when she heard footsteps coming close. For one heart-pounding minute, she thought it might be Cameron, then immediately thought better. He'd be busy at the clinic this morning.

"Need some help with that?" Sam asked, squatting near her.

Jessie scooted from underneath the pickup. "Yeah, I can't make the plug budge. You give it a try, will you?"

She stood up and suddenly fell backward. Sam caught her before she hit the cement floor.

Jessie leaned against the truck, her head spinning crazily.

Sam frowned at her. "Okay, that's it. I'm taking you to the clinic. Something's definitely wrong if you're fainting and falling down."

"Nothing's wrong. Give me a minute, will you? I'll be fine. I just stood up too quickly, that's all."

"Nope, I'm taking you to see McCade. And I'm taking you right now. You shouldn't have a problem going to the clinic now that you're engaged to him. No excuses, Jessie. You stay here. I'll get your coat and purse and we'll take my car."

"But what about the garage? We can't just up and leave."

"Hell yes, we can. I'll drop you off at the clinic, then come back here. The place isn't exactly hopping with customers right now."

Jessie couldn't argue with that and decided to let

Sam play knight-errant. He'd gotten used to "taking care of her" the past couple of years. He was a good friend. He'd teased her about the flowers, but hadn't said much about the engagement. She wondered what he thought about her marrying Cameron.

At the clinic, Sam wouldn't let Jessie just hop out of the car. "You're not walking in by yourself. I don't want McCade accusing me of letting you hurt yourself."

"What are you going to do? Carry me in?"

"If you don't shut up, I might just do that."

Jessie made a face at him. "Right."

He parked the car and Jessie started to open the door.

"Don't even think about it," Sam said.

"Good grief. What in the world has gotten into you?"

He didn't answer, only got out of the car and walked around to the passenger side and jerked the door open.

"Grab you purse," he said, scooping her out of the car.

"Hey, put me down!"

"Not until we get inside and see McCade."

Sam marched toward the entrance, pushed open the glass door and entered the clinic. Thankfully, the waiting room was empty. Sam strode to the admissions window and tapped on the glass.

The nurse opened the window and gasped. "What's going on? What's wrong with Jessie?"

Jessie shook her head. "Nothing's wrong, Sheila. I got dizzy–"

"Jess? What the hell?" Cameron came up behind Sheila and frowned. "Are you hurt? Is she hurt?" he asked Sam.

"No, I merely felt dizzy–"

"Shut up, Jessie," Sam said. "She almost fainted at the shop. She hasn't felt well in weeks. I think you need to find out what's wrong with her."

"Damned right." Cameron rushed around the counter to open the door leading to the examination rooms.

Sam carried Jessie into the passageway and faced Cameron, whose eyes were trained on her. She wiggled and squirmed. This was all ridiculous and embarrassing. "Let me down, now!"

Sam handed her over to Cameron. "Here, take her, she's your woman. She obviously needs a keeper, since she refuses to take care of herself. I'm going back to the garage."

"Thanks, Garza," Cameron said.

Sam smiled a male kind of smile that made Jessie want to smack them both.

"No problem," he said. "I know I'm leaving her in good hands. Congratulations. You're one lucky son of a bitch. And if you mistreat her in any way, you'll have to answer to me."

"I know. Thanks, again."

"Sam!" Jessie watched him leave the clinic. He didn't look back, just waved his hand.

She felt silly being in Cameron's arms with Sheila staring at them, a tiny smile playing on the nurse's lips.

"Please put me down, Cameron."

"I don't think so. Sheila, I'll be examining Jessie in room three. Hold any calls."

"Sure thing, Dr. McCade."

Jessie sighed and gave up the struggle. When they

reached the examination room, Cameron deposited her on the examination table. He kissed her hard, then stepped back, the frown in place again.

"I knew you were feeling bad for the past couple of weeks. Tell me your symptoms–*in detail*. Don't leave anything out. Garza looked pretty shook up out there."

"It's nothing," Jessie said, straightening her coveralls after being manhandled. "I stood up too quickly and was dizzy."

When she didn't elaborate, Cameron lifted an eyebrow.

"I'm waiting, Jess. You worked hard for this clinic to be built. You should take advantage of my professional services. God knows you have access to all of my personal services." He winked. "Come on, sweetheart. Tell the doctor where it hurts."

Jessie rolled her eyes and shook her head, feeling the bubble of happiness she'd been floating on expand. "Well, I *have* had an upset stomach off and on. I've lost count of the days. I'm sure it's just the bug that's been going around."

Cameron stepped forward and listened to Jessie's chest with his stethoscope, then moved it to her back and listened there. "Take a deep breath. Any vomiting?"

Jessie inhaled deeply. "Only once. I've been tired a lot lately, too."

"Uh-huh." Cameron felt the glands in her throat. Then looked in her ears. His hands were impersonal and professional, yet she could feel the healing power in his touch.

"Open your mouth," he said.

Jessie sighed and complied.

Cameron examined her tonsils, then stepped away. "When was your last period, Jess?"

Her head snapped up. "What?"

"Your last period?"

"What does that have to do with anything?" she asked with a frown.

Cameron walked over to the cabinet and took out a plastic- wrapped specimen cup and handed it to her.

"What's this for? I'm not pregnant. Why don't you believe me? I've told you–"

"Just pee in the cup, sweetheart. It's quick, easy and painless."

"But I can't be–"

"You have all the symptoms, Jess. Pee in the cup and we'll have our answer in a couple of minutes."

She hopped down from the table and Cameron took her elbow.

"Here, I'll help you to the bathroom."

Jessie jerked away. "I can do this myself, thank you very much."

He nodded and held open the door, smiling as she passed him on her way out.

She couldn't believe he was making her do this. It was a waste of time. As she collected the specimen, Jessie tried to think when she'd had her last period. What with all the commotion in her life and being sick as a dog, she hadn't noticed. She wasn't regular by any means, but as she counted the days, she realized she was later than usual.

Cameron was waiting outside the restroom when she

emerged and took the cup. "Sit there while I run the test." He pointed to a chair near the scales. "Sheila's going to weigh you and take your blood pressure."

Jessie sighed. "You know this is a waste of time. I have a bug, that's all."

"Humor me, Jess."

She watched him walk to the lab, handsome and strong in the green scrubs he liked to wear for work. A fleeting sadness settled over her. She knew Cameron truly didn't care if she was barren, but damn, she wished she could have Cameron's baby. A little McCade to hold in her arms and sing lullabies to.

Jessie knew better than to wish for the moon, but she couldn't help herself. Several of her most secret wishes had recently come true. The clinic was up and running. Cameron had come back to practice medicine in Salt Fork. And he loved her and wanted to marry her.

Three out of three wasn't bad. But oh, how she wished she could give Cameron a child.

Sheila weighed her, then proceeded to take her blood pressure. "This is so exciting," she said. "A baby! I know you must be thrilled. And Dr. McCade will be happy, too. He's so good with the sick children he treats."

"Sheila, don't get your hopes up. I can't be pregnant. In all the years I was married to TR, I didn't get pregnant. I'm not–"

Jessie stopped in mid-sentence. Cameron hurried out of the lab, waving a small white strip like a flag, his face beaming. "Guess what, sweetheart?"

Jessie stood abruptly and shook her head. "But that's

impossible. It must be a false reading." She couldn't let herself hope... couldn't let herself believe.

Cameron showed her the evidence. "You're pregnant, Jess. I'll do an ultrasound and a blood test to verify it, of course. But this test is extremely accurate."

Sheila clapped her hands. "All right! Congratulations." She hugged Jessie and Cameron, sniffling and laughing and wiping her eyes. "Oh my, I'm so happy for both of you. I'll leave you two lovebirds alone."

Jessie couldn't stop staring at the test strip. She tentatively placed her hand on her tummy.

"A baby?" she asked in wonder.

Cameron covered her hand and kissed her forehead. "Yes, Jess. We're going to have a baby."

A million thoughts ran through her head, each one more fantastic than the last. Something she hadn't thought possible... *suddenly was*.

Her world had turned upside down. Again.

She felt tears welling up, slipping down her cheeks. She hastily brushed at them. "Damn, I'm as bad as Sheila."

Cameron set the strip on the table and pulled her into his arms. He wiped away her tears and sprinkled tender kisses on her cheeks, nose and chin and finally her mouth. When they came up for air, he reared back and smiled that sexy smile she loved so well.

"We're having a baby," he said softly.

Jessie nodded and laughed. "Thank you, thank you, thank you! You've made all my impossible dreams and wishes come true."

"Not all of them, surely?" he said, kissing her forehead.

"Oh yes, all of them." She planted kisses on his neck, inhaling his scent, loving him more than ever. "Or most of them anyway."

"I'm glad, sweetheart. It makes me happy to make you happy. I'll always try to make your wishes come true."

Jessie looked up at him. "Well, there is still one wish you've never gotten around to."

"Which one is that?" he asked.

"It involves a handsome doctor, a Stetson and a soft bed."

Cameron chuckled. "I think I can grant that wish. Is tonight soon enough?"

She grabbed his stethoscope and pulled him back for another kiss. "Tonight is perfect. I can hardly wait."

ABOUT THE AUTHOR...

Anne Marie is a Texas girl, born and raised. Romance is her passion. She loves to read and write about men and women falling in love, overcoming life's obstacles, and living happily ever after. She writes spicy contemporary novels as well as Regency historicals.

Anne Marie lives just outside of Houston with her husband who is her best friend and her own special hero. They have two grown children, two mischievous cats and one sweet puppy dog. Besides reading and writing, Anne Marie enjoys puttering around in her flowerbeds, going to garage sales, collecting antiques and watching old movies.

Visit her at www.annemarienovark.com.

BOOKS BY ANNE MARIE NOVARK:

The *Diamondback Ranch* Series
Book One: *The Doctor Wears A Stetson*
Book Two: *The Cowboy's Surrender*
Book Three: *A Match Made in Texas*
Book Four: *Lone Star Heartbreaker*

The *Return to Stone Creek* Series
Her Reluctant Rancher
Tall Dark and Texan

Made in the USA
San Bernardino, CA
18 March 2017